"The guidance star is gone," Brandon said, meeting her gaze unwaveringly. "Unless we continue to follow that star we'll be off our course in five hours. We'll never get back to it again. Our trajectory will be completely altered."

"And Mars?" she asked. "Can you see it in the wide field lens? It should outshine all of the first-magnitude stars. It was there a few minutes ago. We could see it so clearly with the naked eye that no magnification was necessary to make out the shine of the polar ice caps."

Brandon remained silent for a moment, still clinging to the hope that nothing extraordinary had happened, when Helen Arcularis gripped his arm tightly and pointed.

Nothing but a steady white light filled all space around them. Gone was their guidance star —gone was Mars —gone was the entire Solar System!

THIS STRANGE TOMORROW

Frank Belknap Long

WILDSIDE PRESS

PART ONE

1

From *The First Hundred Years of the Space Age.*
"In justice to the Security Council it must be said that even in the days of the Great Experiment no one was ever sent out into space to die forgotten and alone."

IT WAS thirty minutes to zero count. All about George Brandon there was a low hum of conversation, but the girl with the deep auburn hair seemed to be desperately trying to arrest the flow of time by not thinking at all.

Brandon knew from experience that the thoughts which gave rise to strong emotion could be kept imprisoned deep in the mind. If you tried hard enough it was no more difficult to keep them under lock and key than it was to repress a sob or a cry of torment.

But the effort could seldom be long-sustained, and the auburn-haired girl was clearly in trouble. Her lips had started to twitch and the frozen stillness in her eyes was beginning to change to a look of stark fear.

She was staring straight at Brandon and for the

barest instant he thought that she was going to scream. But she shuddered instead, quite violently, and trained on him a look of such desperate appeal that he wanted to reach out and reassure her.

We're all in this together, he wanted to say. *That should help, you know—just remembering that you're not alone. No matter how young you are, a complete break with the past can make you feel as if you were putting the whole of your youth behind you. You don't want to give up the shining moments when the past seems as real to you as the present. But the future can be even brighter with promise, and you will make new friends at the Station. You are so very beautiful . . .*

The auburn-haired girl nodded. Although Brandon was sure that she wasn't a telepath and couldn't have tuned in on his thoughts her response startled him. Apparently just the look of sympathy and deep understanding in his eyes had conveyed the message.

He was even more startled when she moaned, tugged at the strap at her waist and slumped forward in a dead faint.

A moment later they were unbuckling the strap and checking her pulse. No one spoke as they lifted her up and carried her out of the passenger cabin.

A full minute passed before the hum of conversation began again.

"They'll bring her back and strap her in again if she comes to," someone said. "I feel sorry for her. If she has to make the trip flat on her back, strapped to a cot, it will be even more of an ordeal—"

"It won't matter too much," another passenger said. "It's not pleasant strapped to a metal chair when the acceleration starts building up."

"It doesn't do any good to think about it," a third passenger said. "We've been cautioned against that. What do you suppose came over her? She looked like she'd seen a ghost."

"Perhaps she did. A ghost doesn't have to come out of the past. There are ghosts that come out of the future, if you want my honest opinion. Cruel, malicious ghosts, without a spark of pity in them. I firmly believe that space is haunted—a breeding ground for ghosts. How else can you account for the strange sounds you hear in space. Creakings and groanings, especially at night. Not a few men have died mysteriously in space, with nothing physically wrong with them."

"You hear all kinds of sounds in space. Metal fatigue accounts for most of them. That's what the experts say and I believe them. A little more knowledge of cybernetics would dispel all of your doubts on that score."

The conversation did not surprise Brandon. All of the passengers were under tension. They were talking to keep themselves from succumbing to panic, saying things they did not really believe.

With an effort of will he forced himself to remain calm. It would have been a dangerous time to let the tragic collapse of a frightened girl blind him to the fact that fear was contagious. When seventy-two passengers were crowded together in a metal-walled cabin with no absolute assurance that they would ever see Earth again someone had to set an example of conspicuous self-discipline. There was a need, in fact, for a good many examples and Brandon would have been the last to claim that he was particularly good at it. Fear was beating its head against the bottom layers of his mind, all right. But there was a streak of stubbornness in him which went just as deep and he was determined to maintain his self-control until the countdown ended.

In another fifteen minutes now all of the doors which had been standing open would clang shut, and there would be a resonance within the big, passenger-carrying space rocket which no one could mistake, shattering all illusions, making everyone aware that there could be no turning back.

In a way, it would be the moment of truth. At such a moment a man could tighten his lips and remain resolutely silent. Or he could say something inconsequential to the passenger sitting next to him, and not let anyone suspect that he wanted terribly to look at the mountains and the sea once more, and the autumn foliage turning from russet to gleaming gold.

He could feel hopelessly trapped or more free than he had ever been before, with new frontiers opening out before him in the gulfs between the planets. But the big truths had to be faced and Brandon knew that there could be no real freedom for the condemned.

For the most part they had fallen silent now, and were waiting in tight-lipped silence for the countdown to be completed and the rocket to rise from its launching pad in an incandescent burst of flame.

Brandon was glad that he still had time to look around him, and observe his fellow passengers closely. All of the men and women sitting close to him were United Research coordinators, accustomed to making decisions which could influence human thinking on the highest creative level. But each of them had developed a psychological quirk which made their own thinking suspect.

Surely the human brain was the greatest of all mysteries! Brandon looked at Ralph Sanford, sitting next to him, and thought: *What has gone wrong? What tiny grain of unreason has clogged the mechanism, turning a brilliant research physicist into a violent-tempered eccentric? He's all wrapped up in himself now, his petty emotional frustrations, his bruised ego, the complexities of his beyond-forty life. It was just blind luck which prevented him from killing Templeton—*

When Brandon shut his eyes he could see the laboratory again and the terrible quarrel and Sanford's eyes blazing with fury as he advanced on Templeton with a steel measuring instrument in his hand heavy enough to have cracked the younger man's skull.

Not only Sanford's face, but the entire laboratory had seemed distorted by epilepsy. But that hadn't surprised Brandon too much, because he knew from experience that extreme violence had a way at times of communicating itself to inanimate objects in the presence of an appalled onlooker.

If one of the redly glowing retorts hadn't been overturned and sent crashing in the scuffle, starting a fire that had to be stamped out instantly, both men would have died, and the most trivial of disputes would have lived on to cast a blot on all of their achievements. It would have been harder on Sanford, for nothing could equal the self-torment and spiritual isolation of a man awaiting death in a prison cell.

Andrew Templeton, sitting a little to the right of Sanford, had won two Nobel Prizes for his work in astrophysics, the second one in 2033. Looking at his composed, sun-bronzed face, the eyes shielded by dark glasses, it was hard for Brandon to believe that he'd become emotionally unstable in a very dangerous way.

Helen Arcularis sat very straight and still directly behind Templeton, her face drained of all color. How beautiful she was, Brandon mused . . . if you had a fixation about beauty that was tragically less than perfect and mirrored the torment of a complex and unusual mind. If she had been the central figure in a Greek tragedy, pursued by the Furies, she could hardly have seemed more magnificent in her determination to remain a lonely martyr, asking help of no one.

Brandon preferred women with a defiant girlishness about them and a special gift for mixing reality with illusion in a sanity-preserving way. It would have been hard for him to picture himself walking arm in arm with Helen Arcularis down a country lane, startling a bluejay with his laughter, or carrying her across a brook over slippery stones beneath sun-dappled foliage. But still . . . it was hard for him to keep his eyes off so remarkable a woman.

Sanford turned and spoke to him then, from the depths of a great despair. "It will be hell for the first month," he said.

"How do you know," Brandon asked, removing his gaze from Helen Arcularis and looking directly at the physicist. "How can you be sure? Just space alone, the vastness and the stillness and the grandeur in the sweep of the constellations, may make us feel the way we would if we'd just moved into a new and more spacious house, and were opening all of the windows wide to let the sunlight in. Earth and all of its torments may dwindle to insignificance when we see it as a remote, blue-green globe, spinning on its axis twenty-five million miles from the Station."

Sanford spread his hands, in a gesture which was amazingly conciliatory for so violent-tempered a man. "You may be right. But I didn't feel that way when the Advisory Council made it plain that remoteness from Earth and a dangerous struggle for survival on a new world might help me, but that I'd be ill-advised to think it was going to be easy. It's pretty terrible when you first study the psycho-tapes. You don't want to believe what they tell you about yourself, but in the end you have no choice. Templeton was in a state of shock and had to be carried out of the cyb computation vault."

"They told us quite frankly that the experiment might fail," Brandon said. "And we were given a choice. Submit to psychological therapy in space or resign from United Research."

"A choice like that," Sanford countered, "is just the same as being asked to choose between living and dying. Would you care to spend the rest of your life stripped of all authority, a faceless man in a multitude?"

"There are no faceless men, even in a multitude," Brandon said. "There are two billion men and women on Earth who know that there is very little warmth and human sympathy on the heights. I doubt if many of them envy us."

"But you wanted to remain on the heights," Sanford said, "or you would not be here. You can't deny—"

Before he could go on a harsh voice spoke from the loudspeaker at the opposite end of the passenger cabin. "In ten more minutes we will be in space. There will be no further delay in the countdown. Remember—you will have maximum safety protection during every stage of the journey, including the best possible medical care if you should be taken ill and require temporary hospitilization. During the first half hour it would be wise to avoid unnecessary exertion. That is all."

Brandon was looking at Helen Arcularis again. Her lips were tightly compressed and a slight flush had replaced her pallor. She was straining forward in her seat, as if she resented the strap which encircled her waist and considered that particular precaution outrageous.

Someone coughed nervously and a few feet from Templeton an elderly woman with snow white hair and tired eyes continued to stare at the loudspeaker with a look of weary resignation. Only the tapping of her fingers on the arm of her chair betrayed her inner anxiety. The girl who sat beside her—her daughter perhaps—was beautiful, with luminous dark eyes, and a slender, almost miraculously perfect figure.

For a moment Brandon was hardly aware that Sanford was talking to him again. "It would be unrealistic to deny that the Station is an experiment in psychological reorientation on a scale that would have seemed wildly Utopian thirty or forty years ago. We've made tremendous progress in the construction field just in the last fifteen years. But you've got to remember that we won't be using thermonuclear safeguards on the clinical level. You can insulate an atomic pile against dangerous radiation seepage. But when you're dealing with the human mind no insulation is going to protect you if the material builds up to critical mass before you can take steps to prevent a blowup."

Just how much, Brandon found himself wondering, were a man's alarmist tendencies—if he happened to be emotionally unstable—the direct outgrowth of a weakness in himself that he was powerless to control? If the slightest emotional frustration could send him into a rage the danger of a blowup would seem terrifyingly real to him and very likely to result in the destruction of the Station. The blowup which Sanford had in mind could only occur if the personality quirk he was afflicted with were to be multiplied a hundred times. But he was incapable of realizing that.

It was almost as if Sanford were saying: *You don't know what it means to want something you must have, and to be told that you're just being greedy or selfish and have no right to even ask for it.*

It was a psychological regression, of course—the angry child, the savage child, stamping its foot in fury when denied a new toy, and hiding in a dark closet to punish unsympathetic parents for their refusal to understand. But Brandon knew that reminding Sanford just how childish such temper tantrums were would have been the opposite of wise. Sanford knew exactly why he was one of the condemned.

It was much the same, Brandon told himself, with all of them. When they were told the truth about themselves it was as if someone had grasped a surgeon's scalpel and sliced into a raw, already bleeding cluster of nerve fibers deep in their brains. They knew where the distortion resided, but lacked the skill and specialized knowledge to operate successfully upon themselves.

Physician, heal thyself! Before you can hope to save others you must have a healthy mind in a healthy body or, at the very least, be sure that the illness you are trying to cure does not parallel your own. That was the crux of their predicament, even though they weren't physicians in a strict sense.

Brandon shut his eyes and the years seemed to fall away and he was a boy again, thinking the tumultuous thoughts of the very young.

Life had always seemed to him mysterious beyond belief, human destiny an enigma within an enigma. He had always been a searcher, a questioner, experiencing awe and puzzlement in the presence of things most people seemed to take for granted. But during the past year it had become worse—bad enough to show up on the psycho-tapes as a dangerous emotional distortion.

He had talked with other people who felt as he did, who seemed to be standing on shifting sands in the middle of a desert wilderness when they contemplated the immensity of the universe and the littleness of Man. But they had not been United Research coordinators.

Despite what Sanford had said, Brandon had bowed to what the Security Council expected of him for only one reason. He desperately needed a clearer understanding of himself and an answer to the most bewildering of all questions: Just how important was human individuality and why did some men value it so highly when the meaning of life itself eluded them? Perhaps, in space, he would find the answer.

There are questions so serious that the human mind cannot dwell on them without becoming enveloped in a kind of protective shell which blunts the sharp edges of reality. But it was curious how often, when that happened, one small part of Brandon's mind remained so abnormally alert he could have heard a pin dropping.

He heard Helen Arcularis draw in her breath sharply

an instant before she cried out in sudden, angry protest, causing him to open his eyes wide and stare at her in alarm. He was appalled by the change in her. She was tense and trembling and looked as tormented as the auburn-haired girl had been a moment before she'd slumped forward in a dead faint. But there was one difference. There was defiance in Helen Arcularis' stare and a total absence of hysteria.

She spoke with such vehemence that her voice sounded amplified, as if the loudspeaker had come to life again. "It's not too late to stop the countdown! We can still save ourselves! They need absolute submission now, and we can force them to respect our demands if we convince them that they're not going to get it. To send a rocket into space with the passengers in open revolt would be too dangrous. You don't take that kind of a risk when you're responsible for the success or failure of a fifty billion dollar project."

2

ALL EYES were on Helen Arcularis suddenly, as if her words had made everyone aware of how unnerving speech could be when there was nothing to do but sit and wait. Hours of waiting in eight minutes by the clock. A lifetime of waiting.

She was trembling even more violently now. But her voice remained steady. "We were given no time to think clearly. When there's a knock on the door in the middle of the night, and you're forced to make a drastic decision immediately the bars come down fast. You think the trap is open at both ends at first, that you can still walk out. And when you discover that you can't a kind of inertia sets in. You're too stunned to protest. They used terror as a weapon. If they were capable of doing that—"

"Make her keep still!" a haggard-eyed young man at the far end of the passenger cabin shouted. "She must be mad!"

Helen Arcularis shook her head. "That's what they'd like you to think. But I'm not mad and you know it.

15

We must let *them* know we no longer believe the lies we've been told about the Station. When you appear to be concerned and sympathetic and act ruthlessly no one is deceived for very long. But in an encounter with evil there is something demoralizing in such a contradiction. It bewilders the victim, makes him unable to grasp the magnitude of the evil."

Brandon knew that she could no longer be stopped, for her underlying strength was too great. But he had the strange feeling that deep in her mind she was hoping that her strength would desert her, that she did not really want to die.

She's kept it locked up inside her too long, he thought. *Now it's all coming out, bursting through the floodgates.*

He saw the tall, darkly bearded man come through the door at the far end of the passenger cabin and stand listening a full minute before she became aware that she was under official observation. She was staring straight before her, and without catching her eye there was no way for him to warn her, by look or gesture, that she was in danger.

She had already betrayed herself and to have shouted to her as the tormented young man had done would only have made the stern-faced intruder more certain that she had few supporters and could be taken into custody immediately.

Could he be made to believe that she had many supporters? Almost without thinking Brandon came to her defense. With time to think he might have hesitated, but something deep in his nature rebelled against a tyranny which regarded emotional instability as a crime. She had surely the right to tell the truth as she saw it, no matter how ill or tragically mistaken she might be.

Brandon looked directly at the intruder, gesturing for silence and raising his voice to make himself heard above the uneasy murmuring that had followed Helen Arcularis' look of sudden startlement. She had seen the intruder too now and was half turned about in her chair, her defiance momentarily subsiding.

"It might be wise to delay the countdown," Brandon warned, with a note of vibrant conviction in his voice that was not lost on the darkly bearded man. "Many of us feel that we should have been given more time to make a decision that must be looked at from many angles and in a calm way before it can be accepted without anger or resentment. Even a wise choice will be resented if a man is told it must be made instantly, and he will not be permitted to change his mind. I don't agree with what Coordinator 7 Y 9 has just said. Modern science has many weapons at its disposal which can be used as instruments of tyranny, but with wisdom and maturity they can also be used to heal."

The bearded man had tightened his lips and was moving toward Brandon now with a look of anger in his eyes. But Brandon refused to be silenced. "A revolt now would be an act of criminal folly. But Coordinator 7 Y 9 can hardly be blamed for speaking as she did. She is only human and if she were not ill she would not be here. We are all deeply troubled, alarmed by the way the Advisory Council used the full weight of its authority to make us feel that an emergency situation had arisen which left us little real freedom of choice."

Brandon closed his fingers on the arm of his chair and shifted his position slightly. "Perhaps they were justified. I do not know. I have complete faith in the Council's integrity. But you can possess integrity and still make a mistake in judgment. Only one thing concerns me now. If a revolt starts it will be disastrous, and there is only one sure way of guarding against it. Stop the countdown!"

The bearded man was suddenly at Brandon's side, gripping him angrily by the shoulder. He was no taller than Brandon, but he was built more powerfully. The bite of his fingers was an ugly reminder that a seated man was at a disadvantage and that the strap at Brandon's waist was an additional handicap.

"If you're wise . . . you'll keep absolutely quiet," the hard-eyed official said, his voice lowered to a whisper. "You're doing their thinking for them. They'll be no trouble, if you stay out of it. I'm going to anesthetize her. I've the cone right here and when it goes over her face we'll have no further problem. To carry her out screaming would be stupid."

Brandon stiffened in violent protest. "It would be stupid to use an anesthetic. Are you out of your mind? It's just about the most cruelly vicious thing you could do. At least . . . it will seem that way to them, even if you don't hurt her. They'll see you do it. Unless you want them to revolt—"

"Would you rather I used physical violence? I could knock her out with one blow, but would that anger them less? *Anything* would be safer than carrying her out screaming."

A wave of uncontrollable rage swept over Brandon, blinding him to all caution. "I hope they revolt!" he said, a hot light coming into his eyes. "I hope they lift you up and batter you senseless. Maybe I'll be the one to do it. I can get these straps unbuckled if I try hard enough."

"There won't be any unbuckling of straps," the darkly bearded man said. "I'm not afraid of that—only of what can happen if they all go into a rage. We'll have to stop the countdown if there's too much fury. You can't blast off with the passengers in a state of wild agitation. When that happens the acceleration becomes more than a minor hazard. We'd have deaths—"

He broke off abruptly, his fingers biting almost savagely into the flesh of Brandon's shoulder. "I'll remember what you said. You hope they'll revolt. You're not starting off so well. But we'll have ways of taking care of that when we get to the Station."

The clinician drew a long, trembling breath. The concession he had seemed willing to make at first to Brandon's capacity for restraint had clearly been withdrawn, if it had ever been more than an illusion.

He swung about abruptly, his hands busy with the cone. He had removed it from beneath his gray space clinician's uniform. But he was careful to keep it on a level with his waist until he was at Helen Arcularis' side.

The cone went over her face so quickly that none of the passengers sitting close to her realized what was happening until she began to struggle. Though the bearded man had said that some kind of a risk would have to be taken the look of consternation which came into his eyes convinced Brandon that her resistance was more than he had bargained for.

She had been plunged without warning into a smothering blackness, but she still fought with all her strength against inhaling the fumes. She arched itself, jerking her legs back and forth and tugging frantically at the bearded man's wrists.

He hunched his shoulders and held her fast, his big left hand moving the cone a little and pressing more firmly upon it.

Something exploded in Brandon's brain. With a violence that was self-defeating he lurched forward in his chair, straining against the strap at his waist until the leather cut sharply into his flesh, and forced him to clench his jaws.

If the strap had snapped his lack of a weapon would not have bothered him. He only wanted to be free, for there was a terrible rage in him now, a killing rage and he would not have needed a weapon to make the clinician wish that he had used the cone on himself.

A strap did snap then, a short distance from Brandon.

Perhaps it was the buckle itself which had been broken by Templeton's straining, for the veins on his temple had swelled to bursting and he was out of his chair before the strap stopped quivering.

For an instant Brandon thought that the enraged physicist was going to leap straight for the bearded man and grapple with him, not caring much whether he killed him or not. But instead he did an incredible thing. He circled Sanford's chair without even glancing at the man he had once almost killed and swiftly unbuckled the strap at Brandon's waist.

"Get some of the others free," he whispered. "As many as you can. I'll take care of the clinician."

Brandon's rage was as great as Templeton's, but he had enough sobriety left to know that a resort to open violence would cost the passengers their lives. Templeton's rage was almost certain to get out of control. But Brandon was quick to realize that he could not be swayed by reason unless he could be appealed to by a plea too urgent to be ignored.

"Don't be a fool," he said, thrusting out his arm so abruptly that Templeton was prevented from turning. "An active revolt now would make the death penalty mandatory. If they remain strapped to their seats just protesting won't endanger their lives. Helen was right about that. The only thing that can save us now is that kind of revolt. If they all start shouting they'll have to delay the countdown."

"I see. We don't raise a hand against the clinician—"

A harsh light came into Brandon's eyes. "He'll pay for what he just did. I'll take that risk. But it stops with a beating and I won't need any help."

Templeton shook his head. "I'll take care of him. Get out of my way. I'll free the passengers myself—if you're afraid to. We'll need help to stop the countdown and we've got just about five minutes left!"

He pushed Brandon's arm aside and overtook the

clinician in seven long strides. His assault on the man was quick and brutal. He sent him staggering backward with a blow to the jaw and grabbed his wrist before he could recover his balance, twisting it savagely. He got his arm around Helen Arcularis' waist and freed her, easing her to the floor with his free arm, without relaxing his grip on the bearded man's wrist.

Then he sent his fist smashing into the clinician's jaw again, gripped him by the shoulders with wiry fingers and threw him to the floor. He was on him in an instant, raining blows on his face and both sides of his head until he flattened out with a sobbing moan and lay still. Templeton's fist gleamed redly in the light of the overhead lamps as he got quickly to his feet. He was breathing harshly and his neck muscles were corded into knots and stood out like bony ridges on both sides of his throat. The dark glasses were still securely in place, as if they had been riveted to the bridge of his nose too firmly for violence of any kind to dislodge.

A wave of respect and admiration for the man swept over Brandon for an instant, but he did not allow it to blind him to the criminal folly of what Templeton was planning to do. To have jeopardized his own life was of no great importance, if he no longer felt that he wanted to go on living because of what the psycho-tapes had revealed about him. He had every right to make that choice of his own free will. It was a risk that Brandon had been prepared to take himself, although he would not have battered the clinician quite so savagely and he did want to go on living.

Quite possibly the clinician would not wake up, and Brandon had no right at all to free the passengers now and condemn them to certain death.

For an instant Brandon was torn by indecision. If he tried to prevent Templeton from carrying out his threat the countdown would be ended before he could be stopped. It would take three or four minutes at least.

His indecision vanished when he realized that it was too late now to stop the countdown no matter what he did. It was too late for any kind of a revolt to bring about what Helen Arcularis had been hoping for ten or twelve minutes earlier. Templeton was clearly off in his timing, blinded by his insensate rage and stubbornness to the hopelessness of trying to free the passengers and getting to the pilot room before zero count.

He had to be stopped before he unbuckled a single strap.

Templeton was bending to free an enraged-looking elderly man sitting close to the door, whose willingness to participate in a revolt could not be doubted, when Brandon rushed him, gripping him by the shoulders and swinging him about, with a violence so sudden that he was caught completely off-guard.

Before he could wrench free and take a short step backward Brandon's first thudded into the pit of his stomach, half doubling him up.

Brandon gave him no time to recover. He lashed out at him three times, twice with grazing blows to the jaw and one that landed solidly and with stunning impact.

Templeton staggered and almost fell. But he managed to retreat for an insant to a safe distance, shaking his head to clear it and raising his arms to protect his face.

Brandon was ready for him when he started to fight back. He got in one blow that jolted Brandon severely and sent a stab of pain lancing through his chest. But Brandon blocked two more and delivered a blow of his own that jerked Templeton's head back.

The two men were about equal in height and weight, but Brandon had the longer reach. That ceased to be much of an advantage, however, when the dazed look went out of Templeton's face and was replaced by a cold fury. He fought with utter recklessness, not seeming to care how much punishment he took.

It was a lucky blow that terminated the struggle. It was aimed at Templeton's chest but it caught him squarely on the jaw with so shattering an impact that he sank to his knees and collapsed forward on his face. He blacked out almost instantly.

It was not a victory which Brandon could feel happy about, even though what Templeton had tried to do would have endangered the lives of people he had an obligation to protect. Templeton had displayed great courage, and no matter how wrong-headed he had been in jeopardizing the passengers' lives without their consent Brandon could respect that kind of courage. Condoning the act itself, however, would have meant sharing the wrong-headedness and blotting from his mind the concern he felt for the safety of the passengers. That concern was basic to his integrity and he had been given no choice.

Helen Arcularis had not stirred. She was lying almost directly beneath the loudspeaker, her eyes closed and her face strangely composed, as if the anesthetic had put her so peacefully to sleep that all of her inner torment had vanished. But the clinician was sitting up, supporting himself shakily on one elbow and staring at Brandon in stunned disbelief. His face was bruised and swollen and he spoke with difficulty.

"He was going to free the passengers. But you stopped him. Why?"

Brandon felt his anger returning, but he forced himself to speak calmly. "It's too late now to stop the countdown. And if he'd killed you the passengers would be condemned to death. I don't have to tell you that. You're very lucky to be alive. I almost wish he *had* killed you. I came close to doing it myself, so don't feel grateful or get the idea it was your life I was concerned about."

"I won't forget that," the clinician said. "But I'm willing to forget everything else that could get you in trouble—if you don't make trouble for me. I'm not the short-sighted fool you seem to think me. You're still a coordinator and you stopped him from freeing the passengers. That would carry weight with the Council and you could twist things to make it look bad for me. I could make it look bad for you, too—but it's a gamble I'd just as soon not take. We might both be in trouble."

"You want to strike a bargain with me, is that it?" Brandon asked.

"For the time being—yes. A little forgetting won't cost us anything. Probably I'm a fool to trust you, but—"

"You can trust me," Brandon said, cutting him short. "I may be making a mistake, because I don't trust you at all. But self-interest can keep a man silent when he knows what talking can lead to."

Brandon tightened his lips and stared at the clinician steadily for a moment. "Three conditions," he said. "I'm not keeping silent to save myself, and you'd better believe that. Bear it constantly in mind. My only concern right now is the safety of the passengers, and staying silent will enable them to avoid a dangerous risk. If the Council questions them to get at the truth they may turn defiant and say the wrong thing."

The clinician nodded. "I'll bear that in mind. What are the other conditions?"

"You'll agree with everything I say when I talk to them. You'll help me to convince them that to revolt now would be senseless, because we'll be in space and will need all of the self-control we have left. Just the sight of you angers them, but they'll listen to reason if you back what I say."

"What else?"

"Take Coordinator 7 Y 9 back to her seat. She'll come to in a moment. Strap her in, and be damned careful to do it gently. She has to be safeguarded against the acceleration when it comes. No, wait—I'll do it."

The clinician had started to get unsteadily to his feet, but Brandon stepped past him, bent and lifted Helen Arcularis into his arms. She was not a small woman but her body seemed surprisingly light, almost fragile. The nearness of zero count made him move more rapidly than he would have done if there had been a less urgent need for haste.

The passengers seemed aware of that urgency too, for they had ceased to stir angrily and watched him in complete silence as he made sure that the strap at the unconscious woman's waist was buckled securely.

He did not return to his own seat immediately. He walked instead to where Templeton was lying, lifted him to his feet with considerable effort and staggered with him to the seat the man had previously occupied. Templeton's feet dragged. But he was no longer unconscious, and he groaned in bewildered protest when Brandon eased him back into his chair and strapped him in, with fingers that shook a little.

Brandon glanced quickly at the clinician then and decided that if the man were sensible and braced himself against the chair of the passenger nearest to him the acceleration would be very unlikely to harm him.

Brandon had just finished buckling the strap at his own waist when the passenger cabin began to vibrate and the rocket left its launching pad with a dull roar and a blaze of almost blinding light.

3

THE STATION was traveling through space in an elliptical orbit a half million miles in width, almost midway between Earth and Mars. It was two hundred miles in circumference and built like a spinning top, with a rounded summit and a tapering base. It was larger in overall bulk than any of the planetoids in the asteroid belt between Mars and Jupiter and about equal in weight to Phoebus, the smaller of the two Martian moons.

It was a city-world moving through the gulfs between the planets—an eight-tiered artificial satellite with a larger human population than the average medium-sized urban community on Earth.

Unlike the much smaller space platforms of a half-century earlier it was not manned by a dozen worried astronauts whose chief concern was to remain in orbit as long as possible and transmit valuable information back to Earth by means of a complex system of radiation-measuring devices and specialized equipment in the communications field. It was manned by a hundred and five experienced experts in artificial satellite navigation, and an auxiliary crew of three hundred highly skilled technicians. It was also shining and tremendous, a miracle of scientific construction from base to summit —a visionary's dream come true.

Brandon stood watching the Station draw near the slowly decelerating rocket's central observation window. The journey had taken four weeks, but it seemed incredible to him that so much time could have elapsed without filling his mind with memories of vibration and noise and much excited speculation. The days and nights had taken on an almost dreamlike quality. Time had been telescoped in a way that was not unusual when nothing of importance arose to break the monotony of eating, sleeping, reading and indulging in speculations of a largely backward looking and subjective nature. There were no parallels to what the future might hold, and it was hard to dwell on the future without thinking of it in terms of the past when there was so little to base even the wildest of surmises upon.

If Brandon had been less realistic in his thinking he might have experienced no such handicap. But he had always been reluctant to give his imagination too free a rein in matters of vital importance. What was the good of visualizing a future that might turn out to be nonexistent and be forced to endure a disappointment that he might otherwise have avoided? It was better to let events unwind by themselves and not try to anticipate them—unless you were confronted with an immediate danger that made foresight mandatory. Foresight was only valuable when it was based on careful observation and the law of probability, and a future without guideposts was better left unexplored, if there was no way you could supply a single wilderness marker.

It annoyed him a little that Sanford seemed always

to be standing at his elbow, willing and even eager to set up a long row of purely speculative guideposts. Just the fact that they would arrive at the Station in less than four hours had made the elderly physicist alarmingly restless.

"Do you remember what I said just before zero count, George?" he asked suddenly, and without turning, as if he did not want to take his gaze, even for a moment, from the great, spinning top that now filled two-thirds of the observation window.

"Yes . . . I think I do," Brandon said, watching the Station's lights becoming brighter with a slight quickening of his pulse. "Something about how bad it was going to be at first."

"I said it would be hell for the first month. I refused to even let myself think about the second and the third months. But the first month is usually the worst. If you can live through that you've a fighting chance of becoming case-hardened enough to grow a protective shell. Just going through the motions of saying alive helps. Any man who has been in prison for a long term of years will tell you that."

"We're not being sent to a penal colony," Brandon said. "You talk as if we were. We're encased in a protective shell right now. Our problem is to free ourselves. We won't need that kind of protection if we can face the truth about ourselves with maturity and courage."

"Listen to me, George—listen carefully," Sanford said. "The Council is convinced that our psycho-tape readings are unusual. But you know very well we're not psychotic. The tensions and complexities everyone has to contend with today makes a universally shared neuroticism inevitable. Even if a few of us are borderline in that respect—all right, mildly psychotic—there are two hundred million men and women on Earth just as emotionally ill. You've got to remember that a deep-seated neurosis can be just as hard to cure as a border-line psychosis, and is in some respects more of a problem."

"What are you getting at, Ralph?"

"Simply this. The Council is convinced that any kind of emotional crippling or handicap in a Coordinator would be a threat to the entire structure of society. That makes them subconsciously feel that they are justified in subjecting us to drastic therapy. When you start thinking of anyone in that way, even subconsciously, you single him out as unusual. You exaggerate the gravity of his symptoms. Another thing—he becomes an ideal subject for experimentation, because it's so easy to think that if you can cure him you can cure anyone."

Sanford paused an instant, then went on earnestly. "Don't you see, George? Once they are firmly convinced that our emotional illness is unusual and very grave we may be treated like experimental laboratory animals. Oh, the therapists on the highest level will know better. They'll know we're completely sane. But you saw what happened to Helen when a brutal clinician decided otherwise. They are the ones who will turn life at the Station into a hell for us."

"But they'll be under constant supervision," Brandon said. "We can take that pretty much for granted."

"Wait a minute, George," Sanford said, frowning. "Let me finish. We can't take it for granted at all. The clinicians will take their cue from the Council—not from the high level therapists. And the Council has no magnitude of the problem. They're turning everything over to the high-level therapists. I'm not questioning the wisdom of that, only the way that it will work out in practice. The top men are only human, George. They'll be overworked, overburdened. You can't expect perhaps forty high level therapists to check up constantly on everything that goes on at the Station."

Brandon was not in complete agreement with that. But before he could point out to Sanford that it would be to the high level therapists' advantage to conduct a twenty-four hour check, even if they were compelled to go without sleep, the door a few feet behind him opened and two gray-uniformed clinicians strode toward the observation window and ordered the passengers back to their seats.

Brandon stared for a long moment at the Station before he turned, realizing that he might never be privileged to view it from space again.

A prison? In the Station's technological perfection alone there was a quality of dedication and imperishable beauty which made it hard for him to believe that. Surely ugliness could not emerge from such beauty and demolish it, completely and forever.

4

THERE ARE times when space itself seems to con-
spire with the strange and the startling to enlarge the
boundaries of human awareness. Never-before-encoun-
tered aspects of reality rush in upon the individual with
hurricane force, whirling him about in such an incredible vortex of light and sound and color that the con-
tinuity of experience which links the past to the present
and the present to the future ceases to have any meaning.

Men and women stare straight ahead as if hypnotized,
too awed or frightened to engage in conversation, or
they fix their gaze on a single stationary object—a steel
gray crossbeam perhaps, amidst the kaleidoscopic
shifting of colors—and wait for the experience to pass,
as one might await a slow awakening from a dream
that has become almost unbearably dazzling.

The passenger rocket had orbited the Station five
times, with constantly diminishing velocity, and now
hung suspended in space, as motionless as the metal-
encased city-world which towered above it. As lights

flashed on and off translucent, chemically powered cargo capsules carried the passengers across seven miles of empty space to the lowermost tier of the Station. In each of the capsules twelve of the condemned sat or stood, enveloped in a pale blue flickering.

To drift alone through space outside the firm metal walls of a large spacecraft is far more than just an unnerving experience. It can fill the mind with a feeling of absolute panic. On all sides the universe stretches away for billions of light years, and in that vast ocean of light there are no palm-fringed beaches where, beyond the pounding surf, a castaway can throw himself down and await the coming of another dawn, hoping against hope that rescue will not be long in coming. There are no distant ships on the far horizon, no arising plumes of smoke blown shoreward by the trade winds —not even the hum of a far-off, invisible plane.

The experience is only slightly less unnerving when it is shared by a few others, and there is safety and security just ahead, and very little likelihood that one will become a castaway in the gulfs between the planets. It is enough to know that it *could* happen, that even a seven mile crossing from a passenger rocket to a city-world can be, on occasion, an extremely dangerous undertaking. No conventional power source operates at all times with one hundred percent efficiency, and in very small space vehicles there are problems of heat conversion and heat transfer which can only be solved by preserving a precarious balance between energy input and output through the maintenance of a constant vigilance.

Fortunately, when human lives are at stake, human vigilance is not likely to falter. But it has been known to do so, and giant booster rockets weighing hundreds of tons have exploded in space simply because some minor technician has allowed his eyes to blink shut for the barest instant during a moment of critical testing.

Brandon had left the rocket in the sixth capsule. He sat directly opposite Ralph Sanford, who did not speak at all until the capsule was within two and a half miles of the Station. Brandon was still too keyed up to talk and merely nodded in agreement when the elderly physicist said, "The image which a man has of himself is all-important. It is the only thing that can save him in a desperate crisis, when the ground opens beneath his feet and he must have a firm support to cling to."

Sanford paused an instant, then went on earnestly: "We must never make the mistake of thinking that circumstances beyond our control have placed us at so great a disadvantage that we must wear protective coloration. If a lion could change himself into a leopard the chances are he'd become spotted even in his thinking and be almost certain to end up as a chameleon. By the same token it is the height of folly for a man to pretend to be what he is not. It is much wiser to stand out in a sturdy way like a lion than to be trampled underfoot by accident, and a small, terrified lizard, however ingenious its coloration, is particularly vulnerable in that respect. We must never allow ourselves to forget that we are still Coordinators."

There was only one woman in the cargo capsule. She was extremely plain-looking, and Brandon found himself comparing her unfavorably with both Helen Arcularis and the auburn-haired girl who had succumbed to terror and fainted.

It was not, however, just the fact that the woman at whom he was now staring was physically unattractive that had prompted the comparison. It was chiefly the harsh, almost angry way she was returning his stare, as if she were still remembering the role he had played in forestalling disaster and violently disapproved of it. There was a coldness about her as well, unmistakable in the look of complete unconcern in her eyes when they swept the capsule and rested for an instant on each of the twelve passengers. It was as if she were saying to herself:

Their problems do not concern me. They are complete fools, or they would not be here. I am just the opposite of a fool and I made only one small mistake which I could easily have avoided if I had kept my wits about me. If you are clever enough you can deceive the examiners and your psycho-tape recordings will fail to reveal what you do not wish them to know about you. A machine is not infallible. If you have sufficient control over your emotions a machine can be deceived as readily as a human being . . . and there is no limit to human credulity.

That was not strictly true, of course. At best it was a quarter truth, and Brandon knew that if he had guessed correctly as to the trend of her thoughts—he was by no means certain that he had—she was exposing herself to precisely the kind of rude awakening a boastful child experiences when all of its illusions are shattered by the harsher aspects of reality.

A machine was not infallible, true. But you could not bank on the always remote possibility that it would fail to correctly analyze the data supplied to it, no matter how clever you thought yourself. And just by her coldness the plain-looking woman was committing a greater blunder, for a lack of human sympathy on any level was, in the long run, self-destructive.

Brandon glanced at the timepiece on his wrist and began to steel himself for the ordeal which he was quite sure would be awaiting him the instant he arrived at the Station. There is nothing more difficult to endure without resentment than the kind of official prying that takes for granted that a man with the blood warm in his veins is no different from an intricately constructed machine that has ceased to function at peak efficiency and must be set in motion in an experimental way, examined from every angle, and, if necessary, taken apart and reassembled.

He had no doubt at all that he would be subjected to a rigorous screening. They would not be answerable to a higher authority if they kept him talking for an hour, and asked him dozens of impertinent questions. They would be sure to do so, in fact, if only for the pleasure it would give them to see a Coordinator squirm a little. The shoe would be on the other foot and they would take full advantage of the power which had fallen, like a ripe plum, into their laps.

Brandon's temper rose at the thought of it. Minor officials were all alike, and that sort of thing took place even in hospital admitting wards on Earth. A man could be seriously injured and in danger of dying and have to fill out an information blank before he was permitted to relax on an operating table with an ether cone over his head.

Brandon stared for an instant at the vast sweep of the constellations, mistily visible through the translucent shell of the cargo capsule, and wondered why he was allowing himself to be disturbed by such a comparatively minor affront to his pride. The other passengers would have to undergo the same ordeal and would survive it with their dignity only slightly impaired. Why rail against so routine an aspect of human tyranny when the entire human race was exposed to the much more psychologically destructive tyranny of time and space in a universe so vast that it seemed to make a mockery of all human striving?

The cargo capsule was within a mile of the Station now, and all of the condemned were on their feet, staring at a vertical wall of metal that seemed to be rushing straight toward them with steadily increasing velocity. Brandon thought it unlikely, however, that the capsule had increased the speed at which it had been traveling. With the Station so near the intervening

distance was no longer magnified by optical distortion
and the illusion of slow motion which accompanies a
dangerous journey endured with impatience had seemingly been replaced by the equally deceptive illusion
that the capsule was approaching the Station at twice
or three times its former speed.

The terrifying thought that a collision might be im-
minent had apparently flashed across the minds of more
than half of the passengers, for they stood utterly rigid,
staring out at the Station's flashing lights with a look of
alarm on their faces. Others appeared to regard the
swift approach of the shadowy expanse of metal that
loomed behind the lights almost with relief, as if they
had an overwhelming desire to terminate the space-
suspended isolation which placed no barrier between
themselves and the farthest star in the universe.

On the faces of a few Brandon thought he could detect
a look which mirrored the way a man like himself
might be expected to feel if he were swimming up-
stream against treacherous currents on a river of no
return. It was not a wholly despairing look. But by the
same token it could hardly be thought of as sufficiently
resolute to merit a row of medals.

There was a sudden flurry of movement at the stern
section of the capsule, and a clinician with close-
cropped blond hair, intense eyes and angular features
stood up abruptly and made a megaphone of his hands.

"You will leave the capsule one at a time," he said,
in a voice so incisive that it really did not need to be
amplified. "You must be careful to avoid impatience or
crowding. I am personally responsible for your safety
until you leave the capsule. I hope that you will keep
that in mind. That is all."

It wasn't all, Brandon told himself. Just by speaking with such an air of authority the overserious,
possibly well-meaning young man had generated ani-
mosity.

Five passengers turned to glare at him, and the plain looking girl no longer seemed as concerned as she had been. She tightened her lips and anger flamed in her eyes. No doubt, Brandon told himself, it was hard for her to accept the fact that there were regulations which even a self-appointed superior individual could not ignore with impunity.

He was observing her closely, a little amused by the thought and grateful for even so brief a respite from tension when a lean, sad-looking man said in a voice that was distinctly audible from end to end of the capsule: "It is very strange, but death no longer has any terrors for me. I would spare you if I could, but there is no way—no possible way—for me to do that. I am going to blow a tiny hole in the capsule, and when I puncture it the cold will come in and kill us all without pain . . . and very quickly."

For an instant there was a stunned silence as everyone turned to stare at the sad-faced man. No one spoke or moved. Then there was a swift intake of breath from someone standing close to Brandon and a voice cried out warningly: "He means it! Oh, God, stop him before he—"

The plain-looking girl screamed then, but that did not prevent the sad-faced man from rising from his seat and whipping out a small, glittering object which he aimed directly at the bow-plate of the capsule.

Brandon did not see the almost simultaneous movement or the clinician's hand as it came out from under his smock with a weapon just as glittering.

So swift had been the surge of blood to his temples that his eyes had gone out of focus, turning both the sad-faced man and the clinician into weaving blurs for an instant. There was a roaring in his ears as well which prevented him from hearing the sharp report of the weapon which the clinician was clasping.

There was a sudden, unbelievable moment when

everyone in the capsule seemed to become absolutely motionless, frozen in attitudes of horror which made them look like wax figures designed by a master entertainer to create an illusion of ghastliness for the benefit of a thrill-seeking audience. But it was not the kind of thrill which could be prolonged without a backlash of terror that could make a man want to cover his eyes and scream inwardly.

A small red spot appeared in the middle of the sad-looking man's forehead and widened into a gleaming crimson splotch which covered his entire face. He did not even recoil or spin about. He simply sank to his knees with the glittering weapon still in his clasp and collapsed forward on his face. His body jerked convulsively for the barest instant, as if motor reflexes from his dying brain were causing his limbs to resist the terrible finality of death until the last flicker of expiring consciousness had been blotted out.

Not a muscle of the clinician's face twitched as he slid the small, compact energy weapon back into its holster under the loose folds of his smock, and bent above the dead man. When he arose his eyes swept the capsule with so calm a look of appraisal that Brandon was sickened by it. Did the man have no emotions at all? How could he remain impassive when so horrendous a tragedy had taken place, even though what he had done was to his credit?

What he said shocked Brandon even more, for there was nothing in the statement to indicate that he was any more shaken by what had occurred than he would have been if he had just brushed a fly from his face whose buzzing had annoyed him and whose life had been terminated by a vigorous slap.

"I did only what was necessary," he said. "A paranoid's behavior is always unpredictable, but such self-destructive violence is of rare occurrence, as I'm sure all of you know. With unrelaxing vigilance the danger can be guarded against to a degree which would perhaps surprise you. His expression betrayed him before he spoke . . . a full minute before he drew that weapon and aimed it at the bowplate. I have been trained to detect such preliminary manifestations of the urge to kill, and I am not likely to be caught offguard. I say this to reassure you. We were in very little actual danger at any time."

Brandon suddenly became aware that the young clinician was looking directly at him, his gaze both arrogant and accusing. Before he could adjust to the shock of that Sanford gripped him firmly by the arm and whispered a warning.

"Careful, George. Watch what you do and say. That young man is dangerous. He'd welcome the chance to pin a paranoid label on you."

Brandon returned the elderly physicist's stare with a bewildered look in his eyes. "But why? I've done nothing to arouse his antagonism."

"I'm afraid you have," Sanford said, tightening his grip on Brandon's arm. "He could use what happened in the passenger cabin just before zero count as an excuse to blast you down. He could claim you triggered all of the violence."

"But he wasn't there."

"You can be sure he knows exactly what happened and how easy it would be to submit an official report that would distort what actually took place. You may as well face it. When you came to Helen's aid you made more than one dangerous enemy. The bargain you forced that bearded sadist to agree to must have infuriated him. He may have agreed to keep silent to save his own skin, but that doesn't mean he hasn't done some talking. He'd be unlikely to keep his rage and frustration under wraps when it would be so easy for him to have a quiet talk with another clinician, pledge him to secrecy, and suggest a possible way of evening the score. That's why I'm warning you to be careful. A repetition of what just happened could be made to look like the blasting down of another paranoid killer. All he'd need would be some small reckless move on your part—the slightest questioning of his authority—and he'd have an excuse to blow off your head."

"But he has no *reason* to hate me," Brandon protested. "Not that much anyway."

"That's where you're mistaken," Sanford said. "He has every reason. When a man is greedy for power and there are restrictions on what he is permitted to do it is easy for him to hate anyone who defies and gets the better of another petty tyrant he can readily identify with himself."

Brandon stood very still, wondering just how close to the truth Sanford had come. Seemingly he had come alarmingly close, for the youthful clinician was staring at him now as if he would have liked to talk to the passengers in the same calm way about another dead man whose maniacal destructiveness was no longer to be feared.

Brandon forced himself to remain calm. In three more minutes, at most, the capsule would make contact with the towering wall of metal that still seemed to be rushing straight toward them with constantly increasing velocity and the clinician would almost certainly be under too much strain to risk the kind of gamble that might turn out very badly for himself. The blasting down of two men before one of them had grown cold would be very hard to justify, despite what Sanford had said, and Brandon did not think the young clinician was quite that much of a fool.

In fact, he had already withdrawn his gaze from Brandon and was speaking in urgent tones to the passengers standing close to him, three of whom were displaying too much eagerness to be the first to disembark.

Brandon had seen both blueprints and photographs of the transfer slip mechanism and knew precisely how it operated. It was located in the center of a thin strip of manipulative devices that controlled and regulated cargo intake at the base of the Station. It consisted of a narrow tube seventy feet in length which was vacuum-sealed at both ends. When the cargo capsules arrived at the Station a panel glided open to permit the insertion of a small projecting airlock mechanism into the vacuum. The passengers passed directly into the larger tube and ascended a slight incline until they were standing under a wide expanse of metal that mirrored all the stars of space. Then they ascended six short steps and the vacuum-sealed termination of the tube was converted into another airlock by the swift opening and widening of an irislike mechanism which operated with the utmost precision. Just beyond that inner airlock there was a heavy door of translucent crystal and when the passengers passed through it in single file they found themselves in a large, blank-walled room inside the Station, where admission and processing procedures claimed all of their attention. There it was hard for them to avoid feeling, for the moment at least, that they had ceased to exist as individuals.

Brandon felt Sanford's hand tightening on his arm again. "I don't think the interrogation will take long," he said. "We'll survive it—if we just keep our heads. They didn't bring us here to pile up complications for themselves right at the start."

"We'll see," Brandon said. As he spoke the capsule came to a sudden, almost jolting halt and a sound that resembled a great sigh went up from the passengers.

Brandon looked up and saw that, like a ship, the Station bore its name emblazoned in luminous letters on its hull—*The Molidor.*

5

THE APARTMENT was incredibly spacious, and Brandon was both amazed and bewildered by the splendor of its furnishing, and the miraculous way it was lighted, with lamps embedded in the walls and ceiling that provided a "just right" kind of illumination, neither garish nor oversubdued.

He had never expected anything quite so magnificent and he was seized with a sudden feeling of gratefulness and relief. Not only had the interrogation ordeal been brief and conducted with a courtesy bordering on deference—they had not forgotten, apparently, that he was still a Coordinator accustomed to gracious living.

No expense had been spared to make him feel that his journey had not deprived him of the basic privileges he had enjoyed on Earth while exercising the duties of his high office, and a gladness came upon him which he made no attempt to balance against the harshness and the uncertainty of the long days and nights in space, for he feared that if he did so the scales would dip heavily against his right to rejoice at all.

He was surrounded by the best that twenty-first century technology could provide—the very best, if a man liked furnishings which were as beautiful as they were functional and seemed designed to make him feel that he had not stepped a foot outside of his own home—and sufficient for the moment was the splendor thereof.

Relax and enjoy this, a voice seemed to whisper deep in his mind. It's all yours. They can take it away from you and lock you up in a narrow cell and make you wish you'd stayed on Earth and become a faceless man in a multitude. Tomorrow they can take it all away, and inform you that they've committed a serious oversight and that this compartment was assigned to you by mistake. But for this one night you can set all of the beautiful gadgets in motion, and relax to the strains of Mozart and Chopin and look at a travelscope and imagine that you're back on Earth climbing a hill bright with the russet and gold leaves of autumn . . .

The tapping on the door was faint, but insistent. He swung about, saw the bolt move and couldn't believe his eyes for a moment. Back and forth it moved, a polished strip of metal eight inches long which could be manipulated from outside, apparently, even though the groove into which it was fitted had been designed to hold it securely in place.

He strode quickly to the door, freed the latch and opened it just wide enough to see the white oval of a woman's face, framed in the aperture and staring in at him. Her eyes were darkly shining, her lips slack.

He opened the door wide then, and she came into the room and when he shut the door after her he saw that her features were distorted by fright. But it wasn't that alone that made him stand motionless for an instant, staring at her, too startled to say a word.

Her hair was in disarray and she was wearing a pale

blue dress, crumpled and loose-fitting and belted in at the waist. She was staring at him almost as she had done in the passenger cabin just before zero count, when he had tried to reassure her and she had met his gaze with a look which had made him feel that she had been aware of his thoughts.

She seemed aware of his thoughts now, for she spoke as if they had been talking together for several minutes and there was no longer any need for her to explain why she had rattled the bolt of the door.

"You've never stopped wondering about me, have you?" she said.

He nodded, not quite knowing what to say and preferring to wait for her to go on.

"There is something you don't know about me," she said. "They've kept it a closely guarded secret—even from most of the Coordinators. You must have been startled to see a woman my age sitting opposite you in the passenger cabin."

"I was—a little," Brandon said. "But I thought you might *just possibly* be a Coordinator. You don't look more than twenty-two, but I've known women of thirty-five who could pass for eighteen."

"So have I," she said. "But I happen to be twenty-six and I was sitting there alone. Would you like to know why?"

"Naturally," Brandon said. A slight smile hovered for an instant on his lips, but it vanished when he saw the look of torment in her eyes.

"I am Anne Rayle," she said. "John Rayle was my husband."

Brandon said nothing for a moment. And when at last he spoke his voice, for the second time within a very short space of time, seemed strange to him. "The man . . . who could see into the future," he heard himself saying.

"That's what they called him," she said. "As if seeing into the future was just a stage magician's feat which would draw a huge audience—if it could be built up in a sensational enough way. The man who could see into the future. There have been many others. I am clairvoyant myself and so was my entire family. But not to the extent that John was. No one has ever been as clairvoyant as John was. He could not only predict the course of future events with absolute certainty, he could do so almost at will."

"The Security Council made no attempt to build it up," Brandon said. "They did their best to keep him from endangering millions of lives."

"Yes, I know," she said. "But John couldn't keep silent. If you had his gift of clairvoyance and could predict when disaster would strike with absolute certainty wouldn't you at least make an attempt to use that gift to *save* millions of lives?"

"I don't know," Brandon said. "I'd certainly consider the terrible risk I'd be running of creating panic on a worldwide scale. If you predict an earthquake, a flood or a famine you have to be very sure it won't lead to a dangerous kind of demoralization long before the catastrophe itself takes place. It is very likely to do so, given the tinderbox potentialities of human nature when disaster looms as an absolute certainty."

"But an accurate prediction *can* save millions of lives," Anne Rayle protested. "A flood area can be cleared overnight, if everyone is convinced that there will be a flood. Entire populations can be removed from a region of the Earth threatened by disaster, if an alarm bell is sounded in time. Even the threat of thermonuclear destruction can be—"

"Averted? I hardly think so," Brandon said. "No catastrophe as final as that can be made less destructive by knowing precisely when it is going to take place. If the future can be predicted with absolute certainty —which I seriously doubt—it stands to reason that nothing that human beings can do will prevent what is certain to take place. If the future course of events can be foreseen there is one prediction that no one with clairvoyant gifts can be permitted to make. He must not pronounce a sentence of death on the whole of humanity. He must be stopped from committing so terrible a criminal act, even if it means—"

It was Anne Rayle's turn to finish what Brandon had started to say. "Even if it means silencing him by taking away his life?"

Brandon tightened his lips and looked at her for an instant before replying. "The Council was not responsible for his death," he said. "He was killed by a mentally unbalanced fanatic. The Council would have taken stern but humane measures to prevent him from making such a prediction. Remember—he predicted with absolute accuracy the precise pattern of more than sixteen major future events. That alone gave him so great a following that if he had proclaimed that the world would be destroyed on a specified day, at a specified hour, a billion men and women would have surrendered to despair and we would have had the wildest kind of disorder everywhere on Earth. We are living in an age when scientific technology alone could enable a demoralized one-third of mankind to unleash so widespread a destructiveness that the final holocaust would descend on a world in ruins. There would be lootings, killings and the abandonment of all civilized restraints."

"How can you be so sure of that?" she said. "In a moment of supreme testing humanity might well experience its finest hour. But even if what you say is true—it is surely a crime to silence a man for speaking the truth."

"If there had been any way of determining with absolute certainty that John Rayle's gift of clairvoyance was as accurate as he claimed," Brandon said, "there might be a great many uncompromising idealists who would agree with you. Perhaps only the truth can make us truly free—even if we must pay for that kind of freedom with our lives. But I'm afraid I might still recoil from putting it to the test. It is barely possible that humanity would experience its finest hour. It is certainly always a crime to repress the truth—forcibly or otherwise. But there may be times when we have no choice."

Suddenly Anne Rayle's eyes had a faraway look. She no longer seemed to be aware of what he was saying. She seemed be looking through and beyond him, as if something distant and frightening was making her forget where she was. Her voice sounded distant too. She appeared to be speaking more to herself than to Brandon, as if the words were coming from a tormented part of herself that had receded backward in time and was no longer present in the flesh.

"If he had known that all human life on Earth was about to come to an end," she said. "I am sure that he would have remained silent. He would have kept the knowledge to himself, even though the burden of not being able to share it with anyone would have made that kind of silence seem like the weight of the world resting on his shoulders."

Her voice trembled and Brandon had the feeling that she was struggling desperately to escape from a torturing web of memories that was carrying her mind so relentlessly back into the past that she was close to the breaking point.

It takes forever sometimes, he thought, and waited for her to go on, knowing how "forever" could dwindle to a single instant of time in the depth of a tormented mind without ceasing to be a bleak eternity.

After a moment the faraway look went out of her eyes and she met his gaze steadily again.

"My daughter will be eight on her next birthday," she said. "They took her away from me three months ago. They said that my psycho-tape recordings had convinced them that it would be dangerous for so young a child to visit, even for a brief period, anyone as emotionally ill as I am, and that unless I went to the Station and submitted to space therapy I would never be permitted to see her again. But that wasn't why they took her from me. They are afraid that she may inherit her father's gift of clairvoyance."

"Did they tell you that also?" Brandon asked.

She shook her head. "They were far too shrewd to let me suspect that the Council is torn by dissension. A revolt may break out at any moment. The Council is so divided that my daughter has to appear to be a quite ordinary child who has merely been separated from her mother for reasons which they can outwardly justify, even though there is not a shred of truth in the accusation which they have brought against me. They fear me—and they fear Betty Anne even more. That is why they used so terrible a weapon to keep me from seeing her."

"But they know that she is John Rayle's daughter," Brandon said. "How can they go on pretending that she is just an ordinary child?"

"The whole world knows," Anne Rayle said. "And that is why the Council must go on pretending—erecting a great barrier of pretense that John's followers would like to tear down, leaving no doubt in anyone's mind that Betty Anne is like no other child. As a Co-ordinator you must have had to deal with some of the problems created by the millions of men and women who have resisted all attempts of the Council to repress the cult which has grown up since John's last prophecy was confirmed. That cult has become so powerful that it is beginning to undermine the stability of the Council itself. But with John's voice silenced a new voice of prophecy is needed to keep alive the memory of what his vision once meant to a world that has lost its faith

in the past and looks to the future as it has never been
known to do before. John pointed the way, made people
everywhere realize that the future was no longer a
closed book, but could provide shining guidance in the
shaping of a new and more creative tomorrow. But
death can destroy great expectations by cutting them
short. And who would be more likely to inherit John's
gifts than his own daughter, a child with a double heritage of clairvoyant talents?"

The faraway look was returning to Anne Rayle's
eyes again, but this time her voice did not change. "She
is not clairvoyant now, but John was not clairvoyant
when he was her age. He was twelve before he had his
first clairvoyant vision. But he was an unusual child—
sensitive and imaginative, with extraordinary gifts of
perception. He startled his parents by behaving with
the maturity of a wise and thoughtful adult. Not always, but there were times when he seemed wise beyond his years. My daughter is like that too, and she
could become clairvoyant tomorrow—or before she is
ten or twelve.

"Do you understnad? That's why the Council took
her from me. They fear us both, but they know that
my clairvoyant gifts aren't nearly as great as John's
were, and that I am less of a danger to them. They
know that as long as they have Betty Anne I will do
exactly as they say. I would die inwardly if I thought
I would never see her again."

Brandon nodded. He was studying her closely as she
talked. One thing puzzled him. How could the Council
hope to completely isolate a child about whom John
Rayle's followers were so vitally concerned? How could
she be spirited away and hidden without some knowl-
ledge of her whereabouts becoming known? Rayle's
followers not only numbered millions—the disappear-
ance of his daughter would be certain to stir so violent

a storm of protest that the Council might well be over-thrown.

Anne Rayle seemed aware of what was passing through his mind, for she looked at him for a moment without speaking, the torment deepening in her eyes.

"In the passenger cabin, just before zero count, I became absolutely frantic," she said. "I suddenly realized that I had made a terrible mistake and that I could not trust their promises. I was sure that if I let them send me to the Station I would lose Betty Anne forever. It was what they wanted—what they had planned on from the first. Just the thought that I was hopelessly trapped, that in a few minutes the rocket would be in space, with all hope cut off, made me turn to you in desperation. Just before I screamed and fainted I felt that, in some way, you might be able to help me. It was pure madness. I realize that now. There was nothing that you could have done."

"I felt that you were appealing to me to do something —anything—to delay the countdown," Brandon said. "If you hadn't fainted I would have tried."

"It would have done no good," Anne Rayle said. "There was no way you could have helped me then, but—"

She hesitated, as if what she were about to say would have to be said quickly, or the determination which she had summoned to her aid would waver and vanish.

"You can help me now," she said. "I'm not likely to faint again and I don't feel hopelessly trapped any longer. There is hope now—real hope. Betty Anne is somewhere on the Station. I know where to search and with your help—"

The startled look which had come into Brandon's eyes made her break off abruptly, and wait for him to speak. Her expression said as plain as words that she feared he might not believe her.

Brandon was quick to reassure her. "I might have

known," he said. "If she remained on Earth her where-
about would be much harder to conceal. They can keep
her here as long as they wish, and make doubly certain
of you. And you're thinking that we can—"

"I know we can," she said, without waiting for him to
go on. "I came straight to this compartment as soon I
was sure that whatever happens in the next few days
we will not be separated for any length of time. I had
no trouble at all in locating you, because I knew exactly where to search for the living quarters which I
knew they would assign to you."

"How did you know?" Brandon asked, feeling as if
the universe had reeled a little.

"Because I felt that I *had* to know," she said. "Because I tried very hard to let nothing stand in the way.
To a telepath it is easier to anticipate what someone
is going to do than to look through and beyond the walls
of a room. I probed a dozen minds until I came to the
right one. In one of those minds the quarters to which
you were about to be assigned were as clear to me as a
pointing arrow would have been. It was simple as that—
except that to a telepath the mysterious powers of the
mind are the opposite of simple when they signal you
forward and then call a sudden halt. There is usually a
slight impediment, a difficulty to be overcome. But this
time the vision was swift and sure."

There was a silence, during which Brandon's eyes
swept the room, as if he could not quite believe that
they had not turned to glass and he had become visible
to her from a great distance as she had threaded the
corridors of the Station in search of him.

But it was not really that which was occupying his
thoughts. A sudden doubt had swept into his mind, and
he could not easily thrust it aside.

"Even if I help you to find her and we succeed," he
said, "you will still be a prisoner. You will not be together for long. How long do you think it would take

them to search the entire Station, if they assigned a hundred men to the task? Where could you hide?"

"You are forgetting three things," she said. "Two actually, for one of them you know nothing about. The Station is so large that we could remain hidden for days before they find us, no matter how many men they assign to the task. How long would it take a thousand Security Council agents to find a resourceful fugitive in even a medium-sized city on Earth? A month perhaps. And passenger rockets are constantly arriving and departing. There is always a chance that we may find a way of getting back to Earth."

"A chance," Brandon conceded. "But it would be a mistake to count on it. You said . . . there was something else."

"I have friends here," she said. "One especially . . ."

"Then why do you need my help?" Brandon asked.

She hesitated a moment before replying, then said quickly, "John believed that the future can be changed, but only in part. He believed the part which can be changed influences the present and gives us a kind of choice. As I've told you, I am not as clairvoyant as John was, but I know that in the next few days you will change the future for me and Betty Anne, if you will help me search for her. Together we can find her. Without you I would have no chance of succeeding."

For almost a full minute Brandon remained silent, looking steadily into her eyes, wondering why it was that he could feel so confident that she was practicing no deception and yet could sense a danger which he could not clearly define.

"All right," he said finally. "Just give me a minute to make sure there's nothing I want to take with me. I may not be coming back."

6

THE VERY HUGENESS of the room was frightening. Looking out upon space as it did, it seemed somehow linked to the vastness of the gulfs between the stars, an antechamber into which one stepped in preparation for a journey which would never end. About eighty people occupied the room, their heads slightly inclined as if in silent contemplation of the far flung constellations. No one moved or spoke. They sat silent in narrow metal chairs, in ten-column rows, so statue still that they bore a startling resemblance to figures cast in bronze.

The starlight appeared to brighten and diminish at intervals. This puzzled Brandon at first, but as his eyes became accustomed to the uncertain light he could see that the glimmer cast by the constellations on the huge room's observation wall was influenced by the Station's constantly changing position in space. Constellations in the center of the wall were moving from right to left, and as they approached the edge they vanished abruptly and reappeared a few seconds later moving from left to right. The star blaze was never constant, for at no one time were the same number of stars visible to the naked eye through the completely transparent window wall.

Anne Rayle was grasping Brandon's hand firmly now and urging him to make haste, to cross the enormous room as quickly as possible.

"All of these people have withdrawn so far within themselves that they are unaware of what is going on about them," she whispered. "Space therapy has not helped them. It has deepened their apathy, their rejection of life. But there are so many of them that maniacal outbursts occur from time to time. At any moment one of them may be aroused from his lethargy and become dangerously violent. We must be careful not to alarm them in any way."

Yes, Brandon thought, a little wildly. It is always dangerous to alarm the living dead. They do not think as we do, and their emotions are totally unpredictable. At any moment they may emerge from their self-imposed exile and remember the burial rites that preceded their descent into the darkness, the psycho-tape recordings, the tormenting questions they were compelled to answer before negativism took complete possession of their minds.

There is no withdrawal so complete, no retreat into the darkness so drastic that it cannot be reversed. But the reversal is not always a healthy sign. It may be accompanied by a blind fury, a maniacal urge to seek another kind of escape.

The huge room and its occupants directly confirmed what Anne Rayle had wanted Brandon to see with his own eyes. Space therapy was not always a success. Remoteness from Earth and the vast sweep of the constellations was not unlike a two-edged sword. It could sweep away the cobwebs for some, but it could also heighten the kind of inner torment that Brandon had experienced from boyhood. Enlarge the boundaries of a prison and the inmates may feel at first that they have been set free. But the confining walls still remain, and no one has ever succeeded in escaping from the great prison of the universe.

The huge room's eighty occupants had certainly not been catatonic on Earth. Space therapy had not only failed to heal them. It had caused them to turn their faces to the window wall and resort at times to repetitive speech and actions, compulsive moments and suicidal or homicidal attempts.

Brandon had a sudden, inward vision, startlingly clear, of other enormous rooms which he had not entered—rooms occupied by men and women who were quite unlike the lethargic figures of the living dead who seemed caught up in a kind of suspension between sleeping and waking.

Mental unbalance could take many forms, and now in his mind's eye vision he saw the *others*. Pale, agitated, with drops of sweat on their brows they sat staring out into space with nothing but anger in their eyes. Between the long rows of chairs tight-lipped clinicians were stationed at intervals, anesthetic cones in readiness, prepared to cope with outbursts of violence which had to be risked if space therapy were not to become a hollow mockery.

Brandon blinked and the disturbing mind's eye vision was gone. But the torturing concern and uneasiness which had come upon him did not vanish, for the catatonic withdrawal cases were the most pitiful of all, and there was a grim irony in their plight as well. It had been hoped that remoteness from Earth and a drastic environmental change would diminish their anxiety and their inability to cope with the harsher aspects of reality. But the stillness of space and the glow of a hundred million stars had exerted a kind of hypnotic spell which deepened their trancelike inertia and caused them to withdraw even further within themselves. But they needed to be stirred from their lethargy by an enormous challenge that was completely new, and that would not send them into a maniacal rage. But where on the Station was such a challenge to be found?

"The clinicians may return at any moment," Anne Rayle said, tugging urgently at Brandon's arm. "We'll have to hurry."

"I know," Brandon said. "We've been lucky so far. I should think these cases would be under constant clinical supervision."

"When no one is guarding them they are less likely to become dangerously agitated." Anne Rayle's voice was strained. "The clinicians try to make them feel that they are free to do as they please. They seem to know when they are not being watched."

She paused an instant, then whispered with sharp concern in her voice. "We're not likely to be caught completely offguard. I knew we would find no clinicians here. My mind flashed no warning. There are times when I can be certain, when I'd know instantly if there was any—"

"All right," Brandon said, cutting her short. "I'm afraid I'm not quite as confident as you are. Even if we're forewarned, we just don't know what may happen. How about the next room?"

"I saw it hazily for an instant," Anne said. "I'm trying very hard to keep my mind receptive. Clairvoyant visions come and go at intervals. It's as if something in the mind flashes a secret signal or turns a mysterious key. The next room seems to be unguarded, and it may even be deserted. But I can't be sure of that. There was a slight stir of movement there, as though someone were moving about in shadows."

"And beyond the next room?"

"We'll just have a wide, semicircular corridor to cross," Anne Rayle said, "before we get to—"

An anguished look came into her eyes. "My daughter is not alone. There is a man and a woman with her. I cannot see their faces, but the woman is dressed in white. A nurse, I think. The room is quite small."

"All right," Brandon said. "We'd better cross this room between the second and third row of chairs. The space there seems to be a little wider. I'll go first."

She nodded and released her tight grip on his arm, letting him precede her.

I took them less than a minute to cross the enormous room, moving so stealthily that none of the seated men and women seemed aware that two intruders who were not clinicians were gliding cautiously past them, with a purpose in mind they could not hope to fathom.

The photocell-activated exit panel opened at their approach and closed soundlessly after them, and they found themselves in another room even larger than the one which they had just left. It was filled with weaving shadows and the glimmer of starlight on the window wall, and at first they did not realize that it was completely unoccupied, save for a little man with an innocent, almost childlike smile who stood facing them just inside the entrance panel.

When he saw them his eyes lighted up and he took several quick steps forward and tugged at Brandon's sleeve.

"Tell me something," he said. "Why am I so totally alone here?"

"I imagine you can answer that better than I can," Brandon said, forcing himself to return the little man's smile.

"Oh, well . . . yes, I suppose I can. You see, some of us like to stay when all of the others have left and just look out at the stars. They're beautiful, aren't they?

And when you're alone you begin to really understand what the stars are trying to say to you."

"What are they trying to say to you?" Brandon asked.

"That they are as lonely as we are. Do you know how many millions of light years apart the stars are? Do you know how long it would take to travel from one star to another star and embrace it in a warm and friendly way? A warm, friendly embrace in the cold night of space?"

"Do all of the people who were here a moment ago feel the same way that you do about the stars?" Brandon asked, hoping to find a clue in the little man's reply as to just how far the vanished occupants of the room had regressed.

"Of course they do," the little man replied. "There is nothing worse than loneliness. Everyone knows that."

"And they think of the stars as alive?" Brandon said. "Alive—and as human as we are?"

"Of course," the little man said, his smile vanishing. "You're not siding with *them*, are you?"

"You mean—the clinicians?"

The little man nodded, a look of anger coming into his eyes.

"Just say something that will convince him you're his friend," Anne whispered. "Anything—just a few words. He won't attempt to stop us from leaving . . . if we go quietly."

"We have to go now," Brandon said, giving the little man's arm a pat. "We'll come back soon, and look out at the stars with you. Perhaps tomorrow."

"Yes, yes . . . tomorrow," the little man said. "I hate to be totally alone. This is nothing worse than loneliness."

The big room opened on a semicircular corridor lighted by a single overhead lamp which shed a dull radiance over three massive metal doors with less than eight feet of wall space between them.

Anne gestured toward the door nearest to them, and crossed to it without stopping to whisper a warning, clearly confident that Brandon would exercise the utmost caution.

They stood for a moment before the door, staring at the entrance panel, each aware of the other's breathing. Then Brandon opened the door and passed through it with Anne directly behind him.

The room was well-lighted and about a tenth as large as the huge room they had just left. Brandon shut the door firmly behind him and stiffened to an instant alertness, his gaze passing from the tall form of a clinician with close-cropped blond hair and a blunt, square-jawed face to a child of seven with an olive complexion, and large, dark eyes who was sitting on the floor playing with a flaxen-haired doll almost as large as she was. Just behind the clinician's startled, hostile face and bulky shoulders a sturdily built woman with mouse-colored hair stood with her back to the light. She was wearing the white uniform of a nurse.

The fact that circumstances had made it impossible for Brandon to walk into the room armed provided him with no freedom of choice as to what had to be done when the clinician's hand darted to his hip. Brandon leaped toward him across the room and used the edge of his hand as a weapon, bringing it sharply upward and straight across the man's unprotected windpipe. Then Brandon hit him again, just as sharply, on the back of the neck, and stepped quickly to one side. The clinician pivoted about and sank to the floor like a weighted sack. Out of the corner of his eye Brandon saw that the white-uniformed woman had turned and was almost at the door panel. He overtook her in four long strides, caught her by the wrist and drew her firmly back into the middle of the room.

"You're staying right here until we decide whether there's anything to be gained by tying you up," he said, warningly. "I'd advise you not to struggle. You'll only make it more difficult for yourself."

"If you have any sense you'll give yourself up," she snapped, her eyes flashing. "How can you hope to escape? The Station's big, but it's not like a city on Earth. You're trapped in space. They'll find you—even if that foolish woman has friends here reckless enough to protect you for as long as they can endure, not knowing when they'll be exposed and condemned to death. No matter where you go they're sure to find you in the end. I doubt if it will take them more than a day . . ."

"That's better than no time at all," Brandon said, keeping a tight grip on the woman's wrist. "You may think what you wish, just as long as you keep quiet."

"I'll keep quiet. I have no choice. But when they question me I'll talk until my breath gives out. You won't like what I'm going to tell them."

"I don't like what Betty just told me," Anne Rayle said, in an angrily accusing voice. "She was treated harshly and struck twice. We'd better tie that wretched woman up, just to be on the safe side. I'll tear a strip from my dress . . ."

The child had run to her mother without saying a word, but now she had suddenly become the opposite of silent.

"They said I'd never see you again," she sobbed. "They said if I didn't stop talking about you all the time they'd punish me real bad. They said I'd have to—to forget you, Mama. They said you were very far away and I'd never see you again."

"I know, darling," Anne said, stroking her daughter's hair. "But it wasn't true—it's just a cruel story they made up. You can see now it wasn't true, can't you?"

Brandon said, "I'm afraid we'll need that strip of cloth. We can't risk not tying her up. We'll have to tie up both of them."

"All right," Anne said.

"The friend you told me about," Brandon said. "Are you absolutely sure he'll be able to help us?"

"He'll find a way," Anne Rayle said. "I know we can trust him."

7

THE BIG entertainment salon was crowded to capacity. There was a murmuring, a ground swell of voices as Brandon and Anne Rayle moved out upon the revolving stage.

"The spectacle will continue for five days," Anne whispered. "And every night we will have to play the same part—you a painted clown, I a ballerina with thistle-down feet. Do you think we can keep up the pretense? They'll be on the lookout for unskilled performers. You can be certain of that. Fortunately once I took lessons in ballet dancing. I can leap high into the air, soar almost bodilessly through beams of colored light. Leave the stage and appear to ascend into a world that never was on sea or land. But you've had no experience in behaving like a clown. You will have to grin and bear it and it will be very difficult for you."

"A painted-on grin is hardly a problem," Brandon whispered. "It is not likely to disappear. And I can do handsprings, I think. A tumbling clown, well calculated to delight the children."

"If only there *were* a few children here," Anne whispered. "Why must there be only one child—mine. A child who must remain hidden, guarded, denied the joy of watching a hundred tumbling clowns."

"I'll act as if she were here, watching us," Brandon said, smiling beneath the painted-on grin. "I'll pretend to myself that she's down there in the audience, clapping her hands. It should make the problem of putting on a wholly convincing performance less difficult for me."

"Adults like to watch clowns perform too," Anne Rayle warned. "The simple-minded ones will be completely deceived, for their only desire is to be entertained. They are under no compulsion to be critical and take the flying, Valkyrie-like shapes apart. To them the world of childhood is very beautiful—and very real. But there will be others watching us. A mature and thoughtful man or woman can enter into the world of childhood too, and accept uncritically the dream imagery and the magical interplay of light and sound and color. But the clinicians will be looking for something quite different —the careless slipping of a mask, or a lack of precision in the pirouetting of a ballerina's gilded toes."

She spoke as though thinking aloud and Brandon had the feeling that, for a moment at least, she had almost forgotten that he was standing at her side. She had ceased to look at him, as if she feared to see in his eyes a reflection of her own dread.

"They will be searching for us everywhere," she went on, after pausing for an instant to gaze out over the audience. "No one here can hope to escape their scrutiny. It is frightening to know that you are being constantly watched, that your every movement is being studied. A ballet dancer may talk to a clown, may laugh and nod, but it would be dangerous for you to reach out and press my hand or give them some other reason to

suspect we are different from the others. We must not
be seen together on the stage too often."

"If there are not more than two or three clinicians
here," Brandon said, in an effort to reassure her, "they
will be kept very busy. Surely, among five thousand
people, there are many secret lovers. I doubt if a display of warmth would make them suspicious."

A startled look came into her eyes and she stared at
him steadily for an instant. "Lovers? Whatever put
such an idea into your head?"

A sudden flush had crept up over her cheekbones but
Brandon refused to look away. "I said *secret* lovers.
Perhaps we have kept it a secret too long—even from
ourselves. Why should we go on deceiving ourselves
about our greatest source of strength?"

Brandon saw in her eyes what he had been hoping to
see, and to spare her further embarrassment fell silent.
But she refused to relinquish so quickly the sudden,
bright wonder of so incredible a revelation. She began
to tremble, and then with an abrupt, defiant tilt of her
head she rose on tiptoe and pirouetted swiftly away
from him across the stage. But her smile as she re-
treated said as plain as words: *Yes . . . yes, my darling.
I would offer you my lips if I dared, in plain sight of
everyone.*

There was music then, and a rising murmur from the
audience. Lights played across the revolving stage,
blue, red, saffron. The dancers were garbed miraculously in shimmering knee-length tunics that caught
and held the light and clung like spiderweb traceries
to their wildly pirouetting bodies.

The clowns had moved to the left of the stage and
were being swiftly carried into a behind-the-scenes
shadowland which would not emerge into the light
again for five full minutes.

No such variegated performance had ever been
staged on Earth. It was designed to transcend the

boundaries of all conventional art, to present a spectacle entirely new and different that would be as therapeutic as the drastic change in environment which the Station's remoteness from Earth had brought about. Nothing mechanical or monotonous had been allowed to intrude. Everything was synchronized and smooth-flowing, with the actors so attuned to the constantly changing colors and forms that they could improvise in an original and creative way without ignoring a series of genius-inspired cues. The entire performance had been staged with just one thought in mind—to achieve flexibility without the sacrifice of form.

One of Brandon's fellow clowns plucked at his sleeve. "You have to be in the audience to really appreciate how strange and beautiful all this is," he said. "It's like looking into a magic mirror. It takes you completely out of yourself."

Brandon turned slowly, and found himself staring into feverishly bright eyes, and at a harlequin-red nose twice as bulbous as his own. The clown's grin was grotesquely lopsided and he seemed a little ashamed of it, for he covered it with his hand before Brandon could get a really good look at it.

"I suppose . . . it does," Brandon said, feeling suddenly ill at ease. "But I've often wondered if there's any real need for so many harlequins. A hundred and ten. They're traditional in the ballet, of course, but an attempt is being made here to create an entirely new art form—"

"Yes . . . but don't you see? If such an attempt is to succeed the traditional must not be completely discarded. You must have a kind of springboard from which to take off—a springboard firmly grounded in the past. You cannot create anything truly new and startling out of thin air. Here, as far as the harlequins are concerned, the stress is on the almost unimaginably grotesque. We are not true harlequins at all. A harlequin, in a strict sense, is a performer in a pantomime. He wears a mask and is attired in spangled clothes, usually blue and red, and carries a magical wand. We resemble more the circus clowns of a century ago. In what is known as a harlequinade both harlequins and clowns—buffoons dressed as we are—play contrasting parts. But here we are all true clowns, ludicrously madeup, and that, you see, is the departure. Historically we are an outrageous anachronism—grotesque, dreamlike and completely unreal."

"But if the audience does not know that—"

"The audience knows. Most of them do, at any rate. Who has not turned the pages of an old periodical or book and seen full-color reproductions of true clowns? Some of them were world-famous, as late as—well, sixty years ago. There were traveling circuses when my father was a boy, and I'm no older than you are, But in a new art form—a new ballet departure? It seems somehow forced, dragged in—a discordant note. It's so utterly farcical."

"Is it?"

Brandon had the feeling that the other was smiling tolerantly behind his painted-on grin. He had lowered his hand, as if he'd gotten over being ashamed of the grin and had begun to take pride in it.

"Let me tell you something," he said. "There is nothing quite so tragic, in life or in art, as a buffoon—particularly a buffoon who is a fine and sensitive fellow under the paint. And many buffoons are. Make no mistake about that.

"Did you ever take note of how many clowns there are in the paintings of Picasso? Did you know that in four or five of his self-portraits he pictured himself as a clown, with a painted-on mustache and a bulbous, artificial nose? Glance through a sheaf of his drawings at random and you could easily get the impression that he drew and painted almost nothing but clowns. He was aware of the tragedy behind the mask. Laugh, clown, laugh. There is something heartbreakingly tragic about the laughter of a clown."

"But you just said that all this was strange and beautiful," Brandon protested. "Like looking into a magic mirror. Are we, as clowns, a part of that beauty?"

"We are indeed," the clown at Brandon's side said. "The world of childhood is like that, and always will be—new, strange and very beautiful. And this ballet is designed to conjure up—the world of childhood. When we stand on a high mountain, surrounded by jagged crags, it is good at times to look down into a golden valley, remote and serene. But every child is haunted by night fears and it would be a mistake to remove from the valley all of the fiery dragons, or the sad-eyed, tragic clowns. A child's world must contain both. It would cease to be magical otherwise."

The clown-occupied half of the circular stage was facing away from the audience completely now, and in the darkly shadowed prop room forty feet below the stage Brandon could make out huge glass animals, fantastic dolls twice as tall as a man, brightly spangled costumes hanging from pegs, an incredible number of masks, some topped by feathers and gilded crowns, lifelike-looking toy soldiers with electronic-animation wires projecting from their shoulders, some wearing the resplendent uniforms of two centuries ago, and others dun-gray in hue, with nuclear radiation shields encasing them from head to foot.

"The world of childhood is paradoxical, a wonderland of the ancient and the new and the not-quite-real," the clown at Brandon's side said, as if aware of what he was thinking. "If it were not so jumbled up it would not seem so startling and new. The imagination of a child can soar in all directions, for new impressions rush in upon him from all sides the instant he is old enough to toddle. A child is like a little adult in some respects.

Until he is six or seven his mind can absorb new impressions in so vivid a way that reality takes on a new dimension. The past and the present blend and a new world of enchantment comes into existence. And who can say that the world of childhood is less real, in an ultimate sense, than the one we have come to accept as valid because the years have dulled our perceptions and we can no longer perceive the trembling of the veil."

"The trembling . . . of the veil."

The clown at Brandon's side nodded and went on with increasing animation. "Yes . . . don't you see? The thinnest of veils separates reality as we know it, and the miraculously beautiful—and sometimes terrifying —world of the very young. There are times, even for adults, when the veil begins not only to tremble, but to part. When that happens it is a mistake to draw back and be afraid. There may be wonders undreamed of on the other side of the veil. To recapture the world of childhood as an adult is like . . . crossing a new frontier of the unknown. That is the purpose of this ballet—of all daringly new art forms. All links with the past are not shattered, because, as I've said, there must be a kind of springboard."

The clown-occupied half of the stage had stopped moving and seemed to hang suspended in space above a prop room that was beginning to come to life for Brandon in a wholly unique way, as if he himself had created a world of fantastic gnomes, waltzing mannikins, toy soldiers, and glass dragons and set them all in motion by simply willing them to move with a hidden part of his mind. It was an illusion, of course, and he shook it off as the clown at his side moved closer to him, and raised his voice a little to make himself heard above the drone of conversation on both sides of them.

The hundred and eight other clowns had drawn together in scattered groups, and were conversing in whispers, but their combined voices made a continuous, quite loud sound which could hardly have failed to be heard on the lighted half of the stage, if not by the audience down below. It was interrupted by the music, however, and the continous tapping of gold-slippered feet as the dancers pirouetted and rose to miraculous heights and seemed to blend with the melody of the ballet in a far from displeasing *fortissimo*. Was the whispering of clowns, Brandon wondered, not as indispensable to what the producers of the ballet were attempting to achieve as the many-splendored medley of goblin shapes, pirouetting ballerinas, fantastic colors, waving plumes, and bauble-juggling acrobats in iridescent tights.

"Clowns and the world of childhood," the man at Brandon's side went on, as if still aware of his thoughts. "Don't you see how indissolvably linked they are? The comical, the tragic, the incongruously mixed up. There is no consistency, as we understand that term—we adults, I mean—in the world of the very young at all. The past and the present, the breathtakingly beautiful and the grotesque mingle and blend. Everything becomes topsy-turvy, and then straightens out again. Over and over, but each time a new magic appears, a new kind of wonder that transforms every aspect of the dull, prosaic world that we have perhaps made the mistake of looking upon as the real world."

Brandon asked the question then that had been troubling him in a disturbingly persistent way minutes before the man at his side had begun to speak. "How could a ballet like this be of benefit to men and women who are already in full flight from reality? When the human mind regresses to a more primitive level of consciousness there is no consistency in the visions which it conjures up. The dream or fantasy life of the mentally disturbed bears, it seems to me, a startling resemblance to this ballet."

"Superficially it does, yes," the clown at Brandon's side conceded. "But the fantasy world of the mentally disturbed is actually quite unlike the magical world of childhood. The world of childhood is not pathological. It is the real world glimpsed for the first time by a mind that has not lost its capacity to experience wonder. The veil trembles and parts, and the child is introduced to a new dimension of reality. The beyond-the-looking-glass world of Lewis Carroll, for instance, was in all respects the opposite of a fantasy world that lacks a creatively consistent structure—or pattern, if you prefer to use that word. There are, you see, different kinds of inconsistency and no man or woman in full flight from reality could possibly have imagined the Mad Hatter, or the Walrus or the Queen of Hearts. The world of Lewis Carroll was paradoxical and topsy-turvy, but, like the paintings of Picasso, there was about it a superior kind of logic. It was, in other words, a deliberately conceived and executed work of art. No abstract painter could stand off and simply throw pigments at a canvas and hope to achieve anything but meaningless splotches of color.

"Both Lewis Carroll and Picasso were supreme masters—one in painting, the other in the most difficult of all arts, that of the written word. With super technical mastery they recaptured the world of childhood on a completely sane and adult level of consciousness. Picasso once said that only children could truly understand his paintings. He meant that one must bring to them the unspoiled vision of children who are wise beyond their years. He created something wondrously new, and this ballet is designed to cause the veil to tremble and part in just as bright and shining a way.

"To return on an adult level of consciousness to the world of childhood is not to regress at all, for on the slide-rule of human experience the childish and the *childlike* are at opposite poles. What the creators of this

ballet are attempting to do is to replace the wild, irrational, childish flight from reality which space therapy
has often succeeded in curing by an enlarged vision
that recaptures man's lost sense of wonder in the presence of the unknown. That vision is childlike in the
sense that the world of the very young—the world of a
sensitive and imaginative child—is new and strange
and very beautiful, and a never-ceasing source of delight. It penetrates to the very core of reality and, in a
measure, transforms it—strips away its surface aspects
of harshness, monotony and unbearable strain. You see
what I am getting at, don't you? The world of childhood
is so gloriously sane that it has a therapeutic value for
emotionally disturbed adults—as great a value perhaps
as remoteness from Earth and the healing serenity of
the stars. To be wholly successful, space therapy must
take many forms."

The man at Brandon's side nodded, his grotesque
clown's grin incongruously at odds with the look of seri-
ousness in his eyes. "I'm sure that you do see what I
am getting at, for a Coordinator can hardly fail to be
familiar with the heroic efforts people make to follow a
kind of guiding star in the face of almost insurmountable odds. There is an inward voice which seems to
whisper: 'There is only one completely sane path to
true wisdom. You must have the courage to believe that
reality is never as unyielding as the harshness of
everyday experience leads us, at times, to assume.
There are shining mountain peaks beyond the veil—
peaks which you scaled many times as a child. They
can be scaled again, for they are still there.'"

"Yes," Brandon said. "I think . . . I understand.
There are moments of supreme happiness, of sudden
joy, which we seem to experience only when we are
crushed by burdens which we are no longer able to
support. At such moments the peaks stand out sharp
and clear . . ."

The clown nodded again. "You can be sure that the man who wrote *Alice in Wonderland* saw those peaks too, or he could not have enchanted generations of readers, young and old alike, with a vision that penetrated to the magical core of reality as few other works of imaginative fiction have done. The creatures whom Alice encountered on the other side of the looking glass were weirdly wonderful. Each embodied an aspect of supreme sanity in an upside-down world. They seemed to be saying ridiculous things. But to a knowing, and imaginative child—or an adult who has succeeded in recapturing the lost world of childhood—there is nothing irrational about that kind of topsy-turvy wonderland. It is quite unlike the fragmented and terror-shadowed fantasies of a mind in flight from reality. All children, as I have said, experience night fears at times. But night fears and the tragic pathos of clowns are sanity-preserving in the kind of ballet we are participating in here. It is as new and bright and strange, as shining and wonderful, as the world which Alice encountered on the other side of the looking glass. It is a world which would seem wonderful to any child . . . to an Alice, a Susan, or a *Betty Anne*."

Brandon's heart skipped a beat and he stood very still, telling himself that there could be no doubting the stress which the man at his side had placed on the name. Did he know then?

Brandon suddenly realized there had been no need for him to ask himself that question. The clown at his side *did* know and had penetrated his disguise. How else could he have discovered that Brandon was a Coordinator? No—"discovered" wasn't precisely the right word. Brandon could no longer doubt that the man had known all along.

It could only mean that he was Anne Rayle's mysterious friend—the man whose identity she had been so reluctant to divulge that Brandon had not pressed her, feeling that a man to whom they owed so much had every right to have his anonymity respected.

Apparently, however, she had been overcautious, and had kept the secret more closely guarded than she had been urged to do by the man himself, for he seemed perfectly willing for Brandon to know that his clown's role was more than just a performance-dictated disguise. Even now Brandon had no way of knowing what he really looked like beneath his makeup. But he had ceased, at least, to be just another clown who had engaged Brandon in conversation in a friendly way— out of idle curiosity or simply to pass the time until the clown-occupied half of the stage swung back into full view of the audience again.

"You know who I am, don't you?" Brandon said, and was a little startled by the abruptness of the question, even though he had spoken the words himself. He had not intended to confront the other with so direct a challenge before looking long and steadily into his eyes, to dispel every vestige of doubt as to the truth of what he had surmised. But the question had been clamoring so urgently to be asked that he had spoken it aloud almost without thinking.

He was glad that he had done so, however, when the man at his side replied instantly and with no trace of evasiveness. "If I hadn't known you can be sure I wouldn't have been studying your costume so carefully for the past ten minutes. I selected it, you see—and I wasn't absolutely certain that you could wear it without awkwardness and that none of the ruffles would be displaced."

The clown-occupied half of the stage was swinging back into the light again now, and the man at Brandon's side was saying something to him in so low a voice that he could only catch the final words. ". . . be careful. Everyone will be watching you."

Suddenly the light brightened and became garish all

about him and he was staring down at a sea of faces again. He stood very still for an instant, startled by the sudden brightness, feeling himself to be alone in the center of the stage.

Not quite the center though, for the stage was still turning slowly and when he stared straight across it he could see that Anne was still pirouetting about, as if reluctant to be carried into the darkness in the middle of so flawlessly executed a dance.

It was then that the blast came, accompanied by a blinding flash of light. A look of horror came into the eyes of the man at Brandon's side. He swung about and started running across the stage, elbowing his way between the wildly staring clowns.

The second blast was just as loud, but Brandon barely heard it because it was then that the blow descended. The whole back of his head seemed to explode. But he took three tottering steps forward before his knees gave way and he slumped jerkily to the stage, drifting into unconsciousness without pain.

8

HE WAS AWARE of a persistent tugging at his arm before he opened his eyes. Aware, too, that it was the tugging which had awakened him. He lay still for a moment, preferring to keep his eyes closed until more of his memory returned, feeling a dull, throbbing ache in his temples, and not wanting it to explode into unbearable pain.

He was convinced that it might if he moved at all, or attempted to sit up.

He heard a voice that he recognized then, whispering words of reassurance close to his ear. "You're going to be . . . all right. You were struck down just as the firing started. There was wild confusion on the stage and no one knew exactly what was happening at first. And that can be an incitement to a very ugly, meaningless kind of violence to anyone who is mentally warped."

Brandon opened his eyes. Helen Arcularis was leaning over him, staring very intently into his eyes, as if she feared that he would at any moment cry out with pain.

Her solicitude seemed completely unnecessary, because much to his surprsie, he found that he could move his arms and raise his head a little without experiencing any pain at all. He was lying stretched out at full length on a metal cot in a quite small, blank-walled room. There was no smell of antiseptics, or anything to suggest that he had undergone emergency treatment for a very severe blow on the head.

Helen Arcularis' expression did not suggest that either, although there was unmistakable solicitude in her eyes.

"You're going to be all right," she repeated, as if aware of his thoughts. "You were struck a severe blow on the back of your head, and have been unconscious for about three hours. But the doctor who examined you is not alarmed. He is pretty sure that you have suffered only a minor concussion."

"But not absolutely sure," Brandon said.

"It may take several days before anyone can be completely sure that a severe blow on the head can be dismissed as minor," she said. "But if it happened to me, and I came out of it all right and could move about and sit up without pain I don't think I'd worry too much."

Brandon slowly raised himself on his elbows. "All right," he said. "I guess you'd better tell me what happened."

Helen Arcularis tightened her lips, and looked at him for a moment without replying. When he saw how serious she looked a chill foreboding swept over him.

"There was a revolt and it has succeeded," she said. "One of the condemned—a Coordinator whose achievements have been exceptionally brilliant—is in command of the Station. But Anne Rayle is dead."

"A revolt?" Brandon said. "And Anne . . ."

Helen Arcularis nodded, meeting his gaze unwaveringly.

Brandon remained very still, feeling for an instant like a man suspended in an abyss of emptiness, drained of all emotion. Then an almost unendurable anguish came upon him, and he covered his face with his hands.

Helen Arcularis moved closer to him. Her fingers caught hold of his arm. "It's funny," she said. "You think of evasions, all kinds of stupid ways of breaking it gently when you know there's nothing you can do to make it less of a shock. And the fact that I'm almost a stranger to you doesn't help."

Brandon shook his head. "No . . . not a stranger. Don't say that—"

"I'll never forget what happened just before zero count," she said. "But I haven't talked to you since . . ."

Brandon's eyes stared back at her, his lips barely moving. "That doesn't matter. I—"

"You cared for her, didn't you? You'll need all of your strength now."

"Strength . . . weakness. Does it matter how strong or weak you may feel yourself to be when you've lost—"

His voice became choked and for a minute there was silence between them. Then her fingers tightened on his arm. "I know," she said. "Everything changes and what has mattered before doesn't seem to matter any longer—or not in the same way. It is useless to demand too much of any human being or to expect a man to feel emotions he is no longer capable of experiencing. But what if I told you it would be dangerous for a child whose abduction has triggered a revolt of such violence to return to Earth now? Not just any child—but *her* child?"

He started to speak, but she silenced him by tightening her grip on his arm again. "We haven't much time to talk. But I've got to try to make you understand just why that child is in danger because she has become the victim of a distortion in human thinking so mysterious that I doubt if anyone now living will ever *completely* understand it this side of Eternity."

Her eyes searched his face for a moment, as if fearful that he were still too distraught to grasp the significance of a statement so startling. For the barest instant there was a look of doubt in her eyes. But the calm way in which he returned her scrutiny seemed to reassure her, for she removed her hand from his arm and continued in an even tone:

"It would be perhaps less of a mystery if we knew precisely why an occult prophecy can inspire fear on a worldwide scale . . . the most terrifying and destructive kind of fear. Mankind, of course, has always feared the unknown. It would be the height of folly to try to make light of that fear or to tell ourselves that it is simply an atavistic legacy from our dawn man ancestors, for whom the forces of nature must have inspired terror at every turn.

"Why does a child who sits at the bottom of a dark flight of stairs and stares up into the darkness experience at times a kind of mortal terror, as if some great hand were about to reach down and seize hold of him, and squeeze all the life from his small body? Why does a mature, well-educated man, with no trace of blind superstition in his nature, look behind him when he is traveling along a lonely road at midnight or threading his way through a dark stretch of woodland at high noon? Why do some men and women experience the liveliest kind of terror in familiar surroundings when there is absolutely nothing in those surroundings that would ordinarily inspire terror, except perhaps, if one is in the country, an odd-shaped stone or the way the light seems to be reflected back from a distant lake. Why do we sometimes experience the same kind of terror in the city, in the midst of a crowd? Could it be that we have noticed, just by turning slightly, that a passerby has turned to stare at *us*—a passerby with no right to be there at that particular time. A six-year-old child with a look of adult wisdom in its eyes, perhaps, or a man whose beard is glistening with snow in mid-summer. It would be just our imagination, of course, playing tricks on us. But the fear would be real.

"Have you ever known anyone who could consult a fortune teller and stare into a crystal ball without at least a slight shiver of foreboding? That foreboding can become very great at times, particularly if the fortune teller has penetrating eyes and seems to be staring through and beyond you at a shadow out of Time."

Helen Arcularis paused an instant before going on, her lips tightening a little.

"All of this may seem a far cry from what has happened at the Station during the past four weeks and the revolt itself. But to understand why a lonely, frightened child has become a child of mystery, feared by millions on Earth, the heir to a heritage of occult prophecy unique in our age, we must ask ourselves why her father was able to inspire such fear. We must ask ourselves why his every spoken word has continued to echo in the minds of men despite the passage of time. Why was his uniqueness recognized so instantly and why have a dozen conflicting cults insisted, despite their differences, that his voice has not been silenced by death and that he will speak again, and that when he does, man's future destiny—his survival or destruction —will be written large in a firm, bold hand for all to read? The oracle speaks and his words are recorded by cult leaders and a new mystery religion is born. In the ancient world the cult of Apollo had such an ascendancy over the minds of men that anyone who questioned the wisdom of the Delphic oracle could be condemned to death for denying that there was any human problem that Apollo could not solve.

"There are six billion men and women in the modern world but how many of them accept the reality of a continuously changing universe ablaze with the birth of galaxies from great swirling masses of hydrogen gas? How many of them realize that from a scientific point of view an occult prophecy made on Earth is as inconsequential in the cosmic scheme as a single grain of sand would be, if it were to be picked up at random and placed in a showcase, and revered as unique— completely different from every other grain of sand on all the beaches of the world?

"Today we are witnessing the establishment of a great new mystery cult based on the prophecies of one man. It is a dangerous and destructive cult, as primitive as the jungle night. But almost half the world has come to believe that an oracle has spoken and may speak again, pronouncing words of hope or predicting the end of mankind.

"An oracle has spoken and may speak again. But what if the words come to us in the strangest of all ways—not written in the firm, bold hand of a cult leader, but in the large, round, awkward hand of a child?"

Brandon was suddenly aware that Helen Arcularis was gripping him tightly by the arm. "The doctor will be back in a moment," she said. "If he thinks it's safe for you to get up . . . there is someone who can tell you, better than I can, how bold a vision and firm a determination can be hidden behind the makeup of a clown."

9

HE SAT very quietly behind a communicator-studded desk, wearing the clown makeup still, staring at Brandon with eyes that had a strained, inwardly tormented look.

It seemed incredible to Brandon that he had not had time to take the makeup off. If it were true, as Helen Arcularis had just informed him, that he was now in full, undisputed command of the Station it made no sense at all—was monstrous and unheard of.

"Have patience," Helen Arcularis said, as they came to a halt in the middle of the room. "He'll tell you why he is still wearing that disguise. He took it off, and put it on again. He had a reason . . ."

The man who sat facing Brandon arose and extended his hand. "Well . . ." he said.

Brandon stepped forward and took the proffered hand and shook it. No handclasp could have been firmer or warmer, or have matched more the sincerity and depth of feeling which looked out of the other's eyes.

"About Anne . . ." he said. "What can I say to you?

The revolt almost failed through a miscalculation which caused the signal to be given too soon. Carefully as we had planned it, some of us were caught unprepared. It would have been of no great importance, since we won anyway, if Anne had not lost her life. That turned it into a very great tragedy, for all of us and especially for you. It is victory at a bitter price . . . at so terrible a price that it makes me hate, more than I had ever thought a human being would be capable of hating, the cruel way that life has of inflicting pain and demanding sacrifices that plant a thorn that serves no purpose in itself and mocks the very victory that would otherwise be without stain. But if the revolt had failed the whole of mankind might well have lost its brightest hope and I do not think that Anne would have wanted it to fail . . . even if she had known—"

He broke off abruptly and fell silent, as if what he saw in Brandon's eyes had made him realize that nothing that he could say would be of any comfort to a man so stricken with grief.

He remained silent for a full minute, staring down at communicator instruments on his desk. At last he said, "I must have put this makeup on and removed it a hundred times in the past few weeks. It takes only a moment—and I decided it might be just as well to put it on once more, ludicrous as it may look. You see, there is nothing ludicrous about the doubts that Helen tells me you still have concerning everything that has happened. I asked her to keep nothing back, but you're still wondering whether the man who stood beside you on the revolving stage might not have been killed in the revolt. I could be an impostor—not that man at all. Everything that she has told you could be untrue—part of a scheme to carry the masquerade one step further."

"She didn't tell me who you were," Brandon said. "But if you wanted to convince me that you are the man who talked to me on the stage . . . you've succeeded. Your voice I couldn't possibly mistake, and I doubt if anyone could have imitated the way the make-up blended with your expression so perfectly."

"I was hoping you'd say that," the man behind the desk said. "It should dispel a part of your doubt. *Both* my makeup and my voice were disguises, however. I was very careful to disguise my natural voice and I am still doing so. You say that I have convinced you, beyond any possibility of doubt, that I am the man who talked to you on the stage. That is most important and I wanted you to be sure of it. We are one and the same. Now I am going to talk to you in my natural voice and then, if you wish, I will remove the paint and plastic accessories which have prevented you from recognizing me. But when you hear my natural voice that may not be necessary."

His dark eyes rested on Helen Arcularis for a moment, then returned to Brandon's face. "George," he said. "It was only natural for you to doubt. How could you be absolutely sure when the stakes are so high—a new beginning on a new world, a bright new tomorrow for all of us perhaps—or some dark betrayal you could only guess at. There are not too many men and women who can be wholly trusted—when there is so much to be gained—or lost."

"Sanford!" Brandon breathed, and went on staring at the deceptively ludicrous clown face as if the plastic accessories were dissolving before his eyes in shimmering circles of flame—dissolving and running in all directions and leaving the older man's gaunt features completely exposed.

"Yes, George," Sanford said, nodding. "I fear I have worn a disguise from the beginning, even before I put on the motley of a clown. My friends on the Security Council made very sure that it would be a good one —a skillfully altered psycho-tape, which turned a single regrettable incident in the life of an overworked scientist into a paranoid outburst of the most dangerous kind. The quarrel in the laboratory actually took place, but I did not try to kill my friend or he me. The fire which swept over the laboratory was wholly an accident. The quarrel itself did not go beyond a few heated words.

"I came to the Station to find out exactly why Space Therapy has failed. And it has failed. The great experiment in mental healing has proved self-defeating. Too many men and women have returned to Earth unhealed, after spending six months or a year at the Station, under constant observation and restraint and tormented by their own inner doubts as to the possibility of reversing what the psycho-tapes have revealed about themselves. There is apparently some mystery here that we cannot fathom. Space Therapy *should* cure and in some instances there have been almost miraculous cures. But they have been too few and far between."

Helen Arcularis spoke then for the first time. "All of that can wait. You have called me an impatient woman, but is that so bad a quality—in a woman or a man? Impatience can be an asset if one has the courage to dare boldly. Tell him what you have decided. Tell him now."

"Very well," Sanford said. "George, we are going to take the Station to Mars."

Brandon stared, unbelieving. Before he could reply Sanford went on quickly, his eyes kindling as he talked. "The stakes are very high. A new life for all of us, freedom from the tyranny of the Council—or death for every man and woman who took part in the revolt if we return to Earth. The revolt could not be stopped when once it had started. I was opposed to it at first, but when a man has only one life to live he is making a great mistake if he submits, for one hour longer than he has to, to injustice and outrage. And I saw it all around me, daily, hourly—"

"The Commander of the Station is dead," Helen Arcularis said. "He was killed—"

Sanford gestured her to silence. "The Commander of the Station is very much alive and he does not intend to die without putting up a fight. George, tell me something. Before you became a Coordinator could you have told me exactly what the situation is when you are called upon to repair a malfunctioning piloting device fifty million miles from Earth when gravity is in equilibrium with the motion of the vessel and you have to alter your trajectory at the same time, bringing the vessel out of orbit and straight down toward a landing site less than three hundred miles in width. Could you tell me now?"

"I think so," Brandon said.

"You mean you know so. There is very little about astronautical science that would cause you to lose ten minutes sleep if you had a task like that confronting you every morning of your life. I've read every article you wrote when you were twenty-five, and had no way of knowing you'd be made a Coordinator on the strength of your technological brilliance alone."

"Are the pilots dead too?" Brandon asked.

"Two of them are. The third is close to death."

"And you want me to help you pilot the Station to Mars, and you've let yourself believe that I might refuse. Is that it?"

"If you want to be technical about it . . . yes."

"Right now," Brandon said. "I don't care much whether I live or die. Impatience may be an asset, but I'm not sure about not caring. So it will have to be at your own risk."

"It's a risk I'll gladly take," Sanford said. "I happen to believe it's only yourself you feel that way about, and there's only one reality we can be certain of in life. A man who values his own life too highly is twenty times as great a risk as a man who talks like that—if he's the kind of man you are."

10

HELEN ARCULARIS stood very still, her eyes riveted on the view-glass. "I don't understand it," she said. "A moment ago every star cluster stood out clearly. Now there's a strange blurring here and there."

"A dozen things could cause that," Brandon said, stepping quickly to her side. "You'd better sit down and relax. You've been under a pretty severe strain."

She nodded and without waiting for him to stare out through the view-glass she crossed the pilot room and sat down in a narrow metal chair just to the left of the door panel. She made an effort to relax but couldn't. Her right shoulder twitched a little and she kept her eyes trained on Brandon while he made some re-adjustments in the glass.

"It *is* strange," he conceded, after a moment. "I can't seem to bring at least a third of the star clusters into focus. They appear to be growing hazy in a random way—a cluster here, a cluster there, as you said."

"Could we be passing through a dense cloud of meteor particles?" Helen Arcularis asked.

Brandon shook his head, a troubled look in his eyes. "Meteor dust doesn't obscure distant stars to any extent, unless it's accompanied by a meteor shower that would be visible to the naked eye. Even if the meteors were small they'd be clattering like hailstones on the meteor shields. No—that can't be the explanation. I wish I knew—"

"But you just said there were a dozen ways of explaining it," Helen Arcularis protested. "What made you change your mind?"

"I've eliminated two-thirds of them and the rest aren't very convincing," Brandon said.

"In less than three minutes? How could you do that?"

"It's no problem when you can groove six or eight question-and-verification cybs into one rotating unit on a control panel that practically comes to life when you breathe on it. This is Model 899D57 . . . the newest and the best. The cyb circuits can analyze, coordinate, reject or confirm a sequence of closely linked possibilities in half a minute, give or take a few seconds. You just have to think fast and accurately, ask your questions, and the replies come through in a tidied-up way, in one neat package that's labeled 'data tested' in a series of stippled-in dots. There are flashing lights, too—all over the board. Green, yellow and blue, in case you're interested."

"I'm only interested in one thing right now," Helen Arcularis said. "Why are a third of the stars fading out?"

Brandon had spoken facetiously solely to conceal his growing concern and his expression became strained again the instant he realized that Helen Arcularis was even more alarmed than he was.

She had gotten up and was recrossing the pilot room to his side and he decided to make a further attempt to discount the gravity of what he had seen before she looked into the glass again. The stars were not merely fading now at scattered intervals all across the sky. Whole constellations were becoming obscure, and there were new star formations in the lower right hand corner of the glass that he was totally at a loss to account for, unless he could bring himself to believe that the stars could dart about like whirligig beetles in a pool, in a universe that was as unstable as a house of cards.

"A freakish kind of optical distortion could be the answer," Brandon said. "If a tiny, almost invisible flaw developed in the outer surface of the glass it would be very hard to detect and might cause considerable distortion. In fact—"

Helen Arcularis' swift intake of breath caused him to break off abruptly and stare at her in concern. "Not that degree of distortion, George!" she protested. "How long can we go on deceiving ourselves? There are no familiar constellations left—none at all! I thought for a minute I could make out just one—the Big Dipper. But I was either mistaken or it has vanished in a changing pattern of light." Brandon remained silent for a moment, his lips set in tight lines.

"George," she prodded. "I must know. Can you—"

"The guidance star is gone," he said, meeting her gaze unwaveringly. "Unless we continue to follow that star we'll be off our course in five hours. We'll never get back to it again. Our trajectory will be completely altered."

"And Mars?" she asked. "Can you see it in the wide field lens? It should outshine all of the first-magnitude stars. It was there a few minutes ago. We could see it so clearly with the naked eye that no magnification was necessary to make out the shine of the polar ice caps. It looked more like a dot than a pinpoint of light—"

Brandon nodded. "I know."

He remained silent for a moment, still clinging to the

thought that there was a remote possibility that something extraordinary had happened to the glass. But that final absurdity was shattered when Helen Arcularis gripped his arm tightly and pointed.

Nothing but a steady white light filled all space around them.

PART TWO

11

THE MEN and women on the lost Space Station had been
"out there" a long time.

No one on Earth knew with absolute certainty what
had kept them from abandoning all hope and dying inwardly across the years. Perhaps it was the faces of
old friends, constantly present, or just the way Earth
looked in winter and early spring, or clothed in the
russet garb of autumn. It was almost as if they could
still see their younger selves reflected in a mirror that
time could not tarnish, and could draw strength from
the knowledge that their children might someday know
what it had meant to be alive—and young—at the dawn
of the Space Age.

There were people on Earth who could look at them
moving about on a lighted screen and see no contradiction in the fact that they might never set foot on Earth
again.

Their voices came through loud and clear. During a
swift, summerlike thunderstorm their images might
flicker and grow hazy. But only for an instant, and in

91

that miracle of two-way televisual communication a man seated in his own living room could talk to them directly, and they could talk to him.

There would always be people, Robert Cowley knew, who could see nothing miraculous in interspatial communication of a purely mechanical nature. But to him it was so tremendous a miracle that his mind reeled whenever he tried to picture himself sharing the fate of the lost rocket's eighty-seven passengers.

They had been gone for fifteen years now, and Cowley had watched Betty Anne growing up, changing from a rosy-cheeked little girl of seven into a mature, very beautiful young lady. During eight of those years he had been her tutor. But even now, whenever the instruction hour ended, her eyes seemed to stare back at him in desperate appeal.

"Keep trying, Robert," her eyes seemed to plead. "Surely if you try hard enough you can make the men high up in Government, with billions to spend, realize that another kind of spacecraft, traveling at the same speed and with the same trajectory, might succeed in locating us."

There were so many things he'd wanted to say to her in reply. Some of them would have been reassuring, but how could he be completely honest when just the thought of giving her pain was intolerable to him. He might have concealed a part of the truth, of course, but there was something deep in his nature which shrank from that kind of deception.

The *Molidor* had simply vanished, and no trace of it had been found in the gulfs between the planets, despite a fifteen year search. So what good would it do to remind her that billions *had* been spent—and to no avail.

Had the Station disappeared into another kind of space? Just the fact that the televisual link had not been shattered made that seem unlikely, even though it could not be completely ruled out.

What did anyone really know about interplanetary space? Oh, a few important discoveries had been made since Project Apollo and the establishment of a base on the moon had paved the way for a successful landing on Mars. But what was known was like a tiny, windborne grain of pollen dust blown at random across the frontiers of the Unknown. It might alight somewhere and fertilize some strange new growth of knowledge. But then again it might not, for it could just as easily lie ungerminating for generations to come.

Were there traveling bands or zones of energy in space that could whisk a passenger-carrying rocket or space station right out of the solar system and carry it light years away with the speed of light? Or two or three times the speed of light?

There were other things he could have talked to her about, which would have brought her no comfort. *I'm just a professor of history,* he might have reminded her. *On rare occasions men high up in Government may accord history on the scholarly level a kind of token respect. But not as a rule, Betty Anne. They know that I am not qualified to carve up a turkey that has baffled the technical experts for so long.*

You see, Betty Anne, men on the decision-making level are not all fools. Many of them are honest, completely realistic men who know exactly how dangerous the wrong kind of advice can be. They'll listen to the experts—up to a point. But they stay on guard against letting themselves be swayed by emotional appeals which may turn out to be the opposite of constructive.

The instruction period was over now, and Betty Anne had done an incredible thing. Instead of pleading with him with her eyes, or speaking to him directly she had printed out a message on a large sheet of paper and was holding it out in front of her.

The message read: *I want the world to know just how*

much Professor Cowley has helped me. For fifteen years we have been in constant contact with Earth, and we will never cease to be grateful for the efforts which have been made to assist us with all of our problems. But children need a special kind of knowledge, a special kind of understanding. I am no longer a child, but I would not be the kind of adult I am if Professor Cowley and the other teachers had not labored unselfishly across the years to bring us more than the wisdom entombed in textbooks. It has helped me just to know that there is someone who cares and is concerned about my welfare . . . as only a dedicated teacher can be concerned. There are seventeen children here who still need that kind of help and understanding. Do not let so precious a link with Earth be broken . . .

Cowley wasn't as startled as he might have been if he hadn't known Betty Anne so well. But for a moment he found it necessary to blink a little faster than usual, and there was an uncomfortable tight feeling in his throat.

It would have been easy enough for Betty Anne to have turned a little away from him, and made it plain that she was addressing a worldwide audience with an introductory remark, or a simple gesture. But the printed out message was a little more dramatic, if only because it was so unusual and unexpected. Betty Anne could be trusted not to miss a bet in an appeal of that sort.

It was one of the things he had taught her. "If you really want to make people pay attention to you, Betty Anne, you have to be bold and forthright and do the unexpected. That device has been successfully used in advertising for several centuries now. I'm not sure it's a completely worthy device. But if no one listens to you when you have something important to say you might just as well be talking to a stone wall."

It was one of the nonidealistic things he'd taught her.

But now he was glad he'd stressed its importance. Not because she'd paid him a tribute he neither deserved or could have anticipated, but for a quite different reason. Unless he was greatly mistaken the appeal would stand a good chance of persuading men on the decision-making level to double the number of teachers, and broaden the curriculum of the two-way televisual instruction program.

Betty Anne could no longer see him, for she had clicked off the closed circuit which had enabled her to speak to him in complete privacy during the instruction period. She usually did this two or three minutes before the period ended, to enable millions of viewers to watch the termination of each daily session—another propaganda aid which he himself had suggested. There was surely no better way of enlisting popular support for a broadening of the curriculum.

Somehow he had the feeling, even though she could no longer see him on the *Molidor's* screen, that she was still looking straight at him as her image dwindled.

He could have brought her image back, sharply and clearly, by signaling her to click the closed circuit on again. But he was still too startled and deeply moved to talk to her on a closed circuit without a catch in his voice, and the last thing he wanted to do was to speak haltingly. He was sure that she would understand. Tomorrow he would see her again and tell her just how much he—

For an instant Cowley couldn't seem to breathe. It was the first time his thoughts had carried him so dangerously close to the precipice. It's too late now to draw back and try to save yourself, a voice seemed to whisper deep in his mind. Don't be a fool! She can't see or hear you on an open circuit. So say it aloud . . . shout it to the stars.

Tomorrow you'll tell her just how much you love her.
There. It's out in the open now. Too many otherwise

intelligent people persist in torturing themselves by keeping their secret thoughts in a deep, dark prison and throwing away the key. They're unable to unlock the cell door even when it makes sense to do so, perhaps because self-torment can keep the human mind too occupied to think logically.

Betty Anne had vanished from the screen now and Commander Henry Sanford had taken her place. Commander Sanford was seventy-four years old, white-haired and a little stooped. But he was still extraordinarily vigorous looking for a man of his chronological age. He was discussing with a worldwide audience one of the more recent of the hundred and one problems that had arisen across the years.

It never ceased to amaze Cowley how much advice alone could help, when the best minds went into a huddle and devoted all of their energies to solving a technological impasse. Advice couldn't be solidly packaged, of course, and not even the best minds could devise means of sending supplies of food and medicine to a Station that had disappeared in space. But medical supplies could be stretched and the food problem hadn't become acute yet.

The food concentrates would last for another generation at least and by then—

A terrible kind of despair gripped Cowley and he leaned abruptly forward and clicked the open circuit off. In another fifteen years Betty Anne would be approaching middle age and he would be—an old man? In the eyes of the world he would certainly seem old, even though he knew himself to be the kind of man who would age more slowly than the pompous, rule-of-thumb types who seemed to have a positive genius for putting youth behind them before they were forty.

Cowley suddenly decided there was nothing to be gained by sitting in front of the turned-off screen and torturing himself by projecting his thoughts into a future that was far from completely hopeless.

About once a month, with almost clocklike regularity, morbidity overwhelmed him, and he found himself without the strength of will to go on believing that the lost space station might reappear between Earth and the Sun just as mysteriously as it had vanished into space.

At such moments he had to make a supreme effort to draw all of his energies to a focus, and not let himself forget, for a single instant, that despair could be just as demoralizing as stark, unreasoning fear.

Energization was the key. Keep active, meet and talk with people, live for the moment with the kind of restive drive that can keep a man firmly in the saddle if he works at it hard enough.

Cowley got up, walked to the window and stared down at the university campus. The white buildings, spacious lawns and slow-strolling students did not provide the kind of stimulation he needed. There were times when he valued great architectural beauty and serenity more than most men. But right at the moment —no, definitely not.

The faculty lunch room? Cowley put his hand to his face, but not to brush away the perspiration that had gathered on his brow. He had the feeling that there were cobwebs clinging to his brain, sticky and moist, and the gesture was an instinctive one.

The faculty lunch room might provide the kind of stimulation he needed. It would depend on who was there, of course. The faculty dullards could deepen a man's depression, precisely as tranquilizing drugs had a way of doing. His nerves were not jittery and what he needed was a powerful antidepressant.

Just talking to James Hilton would certainly help— if young Hilton happened to be in one of his more exuberant moods. Hilton was not only a remarkable young man. He seemed to know exactly how to communicate his inmost thoughts without giving a listener the feeling that he was being overcommunicative in an undignified and embarrassing way.

Hilton only dined at the faculty lunch room once or twice a week and Cowley was by no means sure that he would find him seated alone at a table at this particular midday, even if he happened to be there. But there was always a chance—

Luck favored Cowley in both respects. Fifteen minutes later he found himself seated opposite the young assistant professor of biochemistry in a secluded corner of the lunchroom. Hilton had just topped off a chicken salad sandwich with a second cup of coffee and could hardly have been in a more relaxed and talkative mood. He seemed genuinely glad to see Cowley and in no hurry to depart.

Cowley ordered lunch for himself and dismissed the waitress with a nod.

"Another coffee for me, please," Hilton called after her.

Hilton began the conversation with a question that startled Cowley a little, it was so abrupt and unexpected.

"Have you ever been troubled by the thought, Robert, that no young lady had ever had so many admirers as your star pupil?"

For an instant Cowley returned young Hilton's slightly amused stare with a look of bewilderment in his eyes. Troubled? It was not a question which he could answer straight off. The thought had occurred to him, of course, and in a deep, subconscious way it must have troubled him at times. But he had never experienced the kind of active torment that Hilton seemed to be hinting at.

Why hadn't he? Probably because when a man is completely sure—

Cowley felt a sudden wave of panic sweeping over him. Had he any right to be completely sure? Had he perhaps been overconfident in allowing himself to believe that he alone had become important to Betty Anne during all of the long, lonely years?

The doubt was a small one, surely. But Cowley knew that the tiniest doubt, instilled into the mind by even so well-meaning a friend as young Hilton, could take root fast, and turn into a horrible growth impossible to eradicate. He must close his mind to any such possibility, he told himself—now, at once.

Even if he could not entirely ignore the question he could pretend to be merely amused by it and shrug it aside. Just that outward pretense would protect him inwardly, for a man could ward off disaster by pretense alone. The mind will accept as truth a strongly insisted upon lie, and by so doing will be given a breathing spell to think of something better to substitute for the lie.

"I imagine she must have many thousands of admirers," Cowley said, weighing his words with care. "No woman as beautiful as she is could appear on the screen day after day without—"

"Exactly," Hilton said, cutting him short. "But not thousands, Robert—millions. The whole world's sweetheart, you might say, if you'll forgive so saccharine-sounding a phrase. To young men especially . . ."

"To any man," Cowley said, forcing himself to smile. "A dotard in his eighties would find her irresistible—on the screen."

"And why not on Earth, in the flesh?" Hilton said. "You can't honestly believe that so much beauty and grace would have a romantic appeal for the young alone, whether on or off the screen. I said 'young men especially' simply because—well, if she should ever return to Earth she'd have at least fifty thousand offers of marriage from men my age."

The pretense which Cowley was trying desperately to maintain began to quake a little. He was so intent on preventing it from toppling with a resounding crash that he did not see the tall figure of Dr. Stephen Andrews, Professor of Astrophysics, approaching the table and was taken completely by surprise when the quiet, gray man said, almost in his ear: "I was on my way to pay you a visit, Robert. Luckily I decided I could do with a cup of coffee first."

Two lucky-accident meetings in one morning would not ordinarily have displeased Cowley. But this was the kind of accidental encounter which was the opposite of lucky. He had no desire to terminate his conversation with Hilton until he was fully in command of himself again, and able to face up, without any kind of self-deception, to what the youthful faculty member had been saying.

He thought of asking Hilton not to go. But before he could do so the overcourteous young man was on his feet, picking up the check. "I've a lecture coming up in about fifteen minutes," he said. "Sorry I can't talk a while longer." He turned to Andrews with a smile. "I hate to hurry off like this. But I've got a few notes to reassemble before I can spell out genetic A B C's on the blackboard for the young lions to yawn over."

"That's quite all right, Jim," Andrews said.

As soon as Hilton had left the table and was out of hearing range Andrews sat down in the chair which the younger man had occupied.

"Apparently you and Jim were having a pretty lively discussion," he said. "I wouldn't have butted in if what I have to tell you wasn't of such vital importance."

Almost immediately Cowley felt the tension which had been building up inside of him subside a little. Andrews had the rare gift of putting his friends at ease without seeming to do so, perhaps because his relaxed bearing and quiet assurance were distinctly on the special side.

"I may be making an unwise decision," the gray-haired astrophysicist went on. "Too many people envy me because I can authorize the spending of a few billion dollars without consulting anyone." A wry smile hovered for an instant on his lips. "That's something, incidentally, which I would never think of doing. But the fact remains that I'm supposed to be a firmly entrenched insider as far as the Space Authority is concerned, with free access to classified information in as many as eight categories. What most people forget is that just one unwise decision could finish me. My influence would sink to decimal point zero overnight, or even less than that."

He was looking at Cowley very steadily now. "I want you to know just how much I'm risking. But I wouldn't take so great a risk if it didn't give me inward satisfaction, so there's no need for you to feel grateful to me. It's just that—well, I've an ingrained emotional prejudice against keeping information of a crucial nature from someone who has every right to be briefed. I not only happen to like and trust you . . . you're one of the few men I know whose integrity would survive any test, no matter how drastic. I'm absolutely sure of that. But I'm still taking a risk . . . because the Space Authority doesn't always see eye-to-eye with me."

Andrews paused for an instant, as if remembering that a man with startling information to impart should make an effort to speak calmly, if only to spare his listener too great a shock. There could be no doubting the sincerity in the look which had accompanied the elderly physicist's words. But Cowley wasn't quite prepared for the revelation when it came, for it was even more staggering than he had imagined it might be.

"The *Molidor*," Andrews said, "is coming back."

Cowley sat motionless, returning the other's look of quiet conviction with a sudden tightening of his throat muscles and an equally abrupt whitening of his lips.

"You can't mean—"

Andrews nodded. "As far as I'm concerned there can be no doubt of it," he said. "But before I show you the photographs the Space Authority has just turned over to me I'd better tell you what makes me so sure. Precisely how familiar are you with the navigational guidance system which the *Molidor* carried? I mean . . . its technical complexities, margin-of-error limitations—that sort of thing."

Cowley swallowed hard and with an effort managed to say in a fairly steady voice: "The technicalities are pure Greek to me, I'm afraid. I only know that it's so efficient a system that very few changes have been made in it since the so-called 'Dawn of the Space Age,' when a space rocket relied on guidance charting from Earth by radar and a radioed-back series of corrections. I seem to recall that the present system was originally called Star Track Guidance."

"Star Track Guidance is a general term," Andrews said. "It refers to the functional principles upon which the entire navigational system is based. The system's chief component, as I'm sure you know, is an instrument called the Stellar Telescope. The Stellar Telescope corrects the mistakes in a rocket's trajectory and realigns it on its course by taking a fix on a star, very much as the captain of a ship uses a sextant as a navigational aid to determine his exact position in relation to the stars when the ship is at sea. The sextant is also a peak efficiency instrument which will probably never be tossed into the dust bin, simply because peak efficiency and permanence are practically synonymous terms."

Andrews leaned abruptly forward and for the first time a slight tremor crept into his voice. "There can be no doubt," he said, "that the *Molidor* was following a star. We can be equally certain that Commander Sanford thought that the fix which the Stellar Telescope had on that star, allowing for a small margin of easily correctable error, was extremely accurate. He would have had no reason to believe that he was mistaken in that respect, and actually he wasn't. The mistake he made was of a more serious nature."

Andrews tightened his lips and remained silent for a moment, and Cowley had the feeling that he was about to explode a bombshell.

"There was only one thing wrong with that fix," the elderly physicist went on slowly, without taking his eyes from Cowley's face. *"The Molidor was following the wrong star!"*

It seemed to Cowley for an instant that he could no longer breathe. Ordinarily such a statement would not have startled him, for there were too many stars visible from Earth on a clear night to make that kind of navigational error unusual. In the gulfs between the planets, when the stars looked, at times, like a solid sheet of radiance even the guidance supplied by a complex and technically accurate instrument could not always be depended upon to offset a mistake in aligning that instrument in just the right way. To eliminate all possibility of error, the human accuracy factor had to remain constantly in balance with the machine at the opposite end of the equation. Let one outweigh the other and the entire equation was very likely to become misleading and of no value at all.

Cowley knew, with almost absolute certainty, that Andrews was not talking about just *any* star. The mistake in navigation wasn't primarily a directional one—couldn't have been. If it had hinged solely on the fact that Commander Sanford or the Stellar Telescope had made a simple error in calculation and picked the wrong star among uncounted millions of stars Andrews could surely have been aware that an error of that kind could hardly cause a rocket to vanish inside the Solar System without leaving a trace. There had to be a great deal more to the explanation than that, and the intensity of emotion which the physicist had displayed left little doubt in Cowley's mind that something extraordinary had taken place.

"Just what do you mean by the 'wrong' star?" he asked, a little more in control of himself now. "Are you referring to a simple error in navigation—the kind that is made a dozen times a year at least? Almost everyone believes that the *Molidor* went astray through some kind of navigational miscalculation before it vanished, even though there has never been anything wrong with the guidance system as far as Sanford has been able to determine. It functions now, he claims, in a kind of vacuum, with perfectly coordinated movements that accomplish nothing at all."

"I'll explain what I mean in a moment," Andrews said. "First I'd like to point out that a system functioning in a vacuum can be perfectly accurate in every respect, if you judge its performance on the basis of the accuracy you'd normally expect from it in the field it was originally designed to function in. For instance, photocells change their electric output when they are exposed to outer space. But they would still function accurately on Earth and they continue to function in a very interesting way in outer space. There is nothing basically wrong with them in either environment."

"I understand all that," Cowley said, a trifle impatiently. "But if—"

Andrews cut him short with an abrupt wave of his hand. "I just wanted to clarify something that seemed to puzzle you," he said. "It has no very direct bearing on what I'm going to tell you. It's of fringe significance, of course. But there'll be discussions on the screen in another week or so that should satisfy your curiosity in that respect."

He paused again for the barest instant, as if he did not wish to be hurried. But when he saw the look of tormented impatience in Cowley's eyes he went on quickly: "You asked me what I meant by the 'wrong' star. I was referring to something so strange—so contrary to what most astrophysicists believe about the basic structure of the physical universe—that I would have refused to take it seriously if some quite startling photographic evidence hadn't arrived from the Space Authority this morning. To my mind, it is the kind of evidence which only a fool would refuse to take seriously."

Andrews raised his hand and looked at it for a moment, as if he would not have been too surprised to discover he had six fingers and that two of the original five had doubled in length.

"Tell me," he said, folding one hand over the other. "Have you ever heard of Frederick Carswell's hypothesis of superimposed suns in overlapping or doubled back space?"

Cowley shook his head.

"Well . . . very few people have. But it's a beautiful hypothesis, in a way. You're familiar, of course, with the ten or twelve most widely accepted hypotheses concerning the precise nature of the physical universe . . . or, if you prefer, the universe of stars. In all but two of them its curvature is accepted as a basic premise, and if the space-time continuum is actually a closed system, space must double back on itself, or overlap in some way.

"But consider this. Even if we accept that premise we'd have no way of knowing just how compact or contiguous that overlapping would be. Most astrophysicists believe that if you circle the entire inner-outer circumference of a curved universe you'll come back to your home planet in the universe of stars. I use the term 'inner-outer,' of course, as a substitute for X, a rind-of-the-orange intangible we'll probably never be able to describe in a more satisfying way. Anyway, if you circle the entire rind, so to speak, you'll see our Solar System again and Earth itself."

"In a journey that would take billions of human lifetimes to complete," Cowley said.

Andrews nodded. "Trillions, most likely. But perhaps you would not need to encircle the rind of the orange in a journey whose duration would stagger the imagination in terms of light years alone. Perhaps the curved universe is folded back upon itself in such a way that star systems at the opposite end of space are actually the Solar System's next door neighbors.

"What if two suns, identical or almost identical in magnitude, exist side by side in different dimensions of space-time, separated by the thinnest of spatial barriers? What if they are actually superimposed—two suns at opposite ends of space if you measure the distance which separates them across the great curve of the universe in light years, but scarcely separated at all if you cut across that distance in a tangential way through the space-time continuum folded back on itself?

"What if the barrier between them occasionally wavers and dissolves? How can we be sure that the continuum always remains stable and unalterable throughout the universe of stars? For all we know the barrier—if Carswell's hypothesis is sound—may turn fluid and run like quicksilver at times. Do you grasp what I mean? That's what makes Carswell's hypothesis so beautiful . . . the possibility that the entire physical universe may be as unstable as a house of cards."

"But Good God!" Cowley breathed. "If it happened often—"

"Probably not often, even if Carswell's hypothesis is

sound," Andrews said. "Throughout the whole of nature how much of that kind of instability do you find? If plants, animals and rock formations dissolved at times like tallow in hot sunlight you can be quite sure we wouldn't be here at all."

"But Earth is only a flyspeck of matter in space," Cowley said. "What you've just said proves nothing at all."

"That is quite true," Andrews said. "It *proves* nothing. But it does suggest, in a general way, that instability on a cosmic scale may be a rare occurrence, if it exists at all. Nature follows a pretty uniform pattern, from the atom to the spiral nebulae."

"You almost had me convinced for a moment," Cowley said. "But what you've been saying is insane. How many astrophysicists do you know who take Carswell seriously . . . or place any credence in his hypothesis at all? Three—five?"

"Just one," Andrews said. "I couldn't have said that before these three photographs from the Space Authority arrived. I think you'd better look at them before you judge me too harshly. No man likes to be labeled psychotic before the brain watchers have looked over his charts and are convinced of it themselves."

Andrews laid the three photographs down on the table in front of Cowley, spreading them out fanwise so that he could see them clearly.

In the first the Sun stood out sharply against the blackness of space, with a clearly visible corona. There seemed to be a faint fuzziness a little to the right of it. In the second there were two suns instead of one, one slightly super-imposed on the other. In the third photograph there was a tiny blob of brightness shaped like a spindle moving tangential to the two suns, far down in the right hand corner of the photograph.

"Good Lord!" Cowley said.

From: SUN OR MIRAGE? *Great Unsolved Mysteries of the Skies.* Gilson. 2234.

The middle years of the twenty-first century witnessed an event so astounding that it is doubtful if there is anything in the swiftly following Martian Colonization Era which more profoundly altered what had previously been believed about the structure of the physical universe and the mysteries of space and time. The Station reappeared, and behind it there seemed to hover, for several days, two suns identical in magnitude and size. Only our Sun stood out clearly. The other sun was ghostly from the first and did not in any way increase the warmth of the Solar rays, although the two suns were almost superimposed. When the "ghost sun" vanished the Station continued on toward Earth for several days, then abruptly reversed its course, and traveled outward into space again. Despite its size, it quickly ceased to be visible from Earth and its destination remained unknown for almost ten years, although televisual contact with Earth continued as before. The secrecy as to its whereabouts was rigidly enforced by Commander Sanford and although the transmission appeared to be coming from Mars there was no way its precise location could be determined with any degree of accuracy.

12

"MAY I come in, sir?"

Brandon turned slowly from the wind velocity recorder he'd been studying for half an hour, recognizing the voice and wondering why it was that the younger generation could make such nuisances of themselves at times that you had to avoid them like the plague to get any work done.

"Yes, of course, Roger," he said, doing his best to make his voice sound friendly. "Come in and sit down. Precisely what did you wish to see me about?"

Young Stearns came into the chart room and shut the door panel firmly behind him. His blond hair glimmered in the overhead lamps and his rather sharp-angled but not unhandsome face displayed a troubled frown.

"Sit down, sit down," Brandon said impatiently, when he saw that Stearns had come to a dead halt in the middle of the small instrument room, and was not even glancing toward the chair that stood a little to the left of the wind velocity recorder. It seemed a trifle too small to comfortably accommodate the young man's big-boned frame, but to Brandon that seemed no excuse for his refusal to wedge himself into it.

Stearns cast a reproachful glance at Brandon, and crossed to the chair in three long strides, his frown deepening as he seated himself. It was a very close fit.

"Well?" Brandon said, letting his hand glide over the smoothly polished top of the recorder as if he wanted Stearns to know that right at the moment the instrument was taking up all of his time, and that he was very much attached to it.

"It's about your daughter, sir," young Stearns said.

"My adopted daughter, you mean," Brandon said, aware that a trace of asperity had crept into his voice which he felt unhappy about. He had nothing against Stearns—rather liked him, in fact. But he'd been under a strain all morning, and Stearns seemed at times to be overenergized—hardly a fault in a young man of twenty-two, but not exactly a point in his favor either.

"If you'll forgive me, sir," Stearns said. "No one ever thinks of her as your adopted daughter. I'm afraid she doesn't herself. When she calls you 'Dad' I'm quite sure she has no reservations about it."

"I'm grateful for the information," Brandon said. "I've often thought more people would adopt children if they could be sure they'd come to feel that way."

"I think you know how she feels, sir. And you're not deceiving me by pretending it's news to you."

Brandon found that he no longer had to struggle to keep the harshness out of his voice. "Well . . . it *is* rather gratifying to have something like that confirmed by a disinterested third party," he said.

"I'm not disinterested, unfortunately," Stearns said. "I'm very much in love with your daughter."

"I won't pretend that's news to me," Brandon said, smiling. "But why 'unfortunately?' "

"Because she's not in love with me, sir."

"I see. I'm afraid that isn't news to me either. She's in love with a man twice her age, and there's nothing very much that you or I can do about it. The fact that he's fifty million miles away doesn't seem to make any difference."

"I can't believe she's really in love with him," Stearns said, quickly. "It's just a kind of—well, schoolgirl idealization. You've got to remember that he's been her teacher since she was a very little girl—seven years old when the telecast lectures started. And nothing has happened in all the years he has been her teacher to disillusion her. It's very hard to overcome that kind of an idealization."

"I know," Brandon said. "He's watched her growing up and becoming a radiantly beautiful young lady. And she's watched him seeming to grow wiser and more wonderful year by year. He's guided her thoughts across the years as not even I could have done. He's more of a poet than I am, even though he's supposed to be just a teacher of history. He has made history come to life for her, in all of its pageantry and splendor."

"He has made a great many other things come to life for her," Stearns conceded. "The sunsets on Earth which she has never seen, the sea and the sky and the full moon shining down on fields of golden grain. Mars may be even more beautiful in other ways, but to a child who cannot remember Earth—"

"I know," Brandon said. "You can see it on the screen in full color, but it takes the words of an inspired teacher to make it seem completely real. The cities too, of course—Paris and London and New York. He has guided her wisely, with a rare kind of perceptiveness."

"You seem to have a great respect and admiration for him," Stearns said.

"Naturally," Brandon said, nodding. "Don't you?"

"I suppose I do," Stearns conceded. "But I can't help

hating him also. Oh, I know that's a black mark against me. I have nothing at all against him, really. But a man in love can be unreasonable and unjust."

"There's no need for you to feel guilty about it," Brandon said. "If I were in your shoes I'd be just as angry and resentful. Circumstances have given him an advantage which seems to you unfair. You feel that you might have won if the battle could have been waged on more equal terms. But aren't you forgetting that you have an advantage also? You are on Mars and he is on Earth. You can see her and talk to her every day."

"So can he," Stearns said.

"But not quite in the same way. You can reach out and press her hand."

"She does not want me to reach out and press her hand," Stearns said. "She stops me every time I try to tell her how much I—"

Stearns fell silent, a look of despair coming into his eyes.

"I'm going to say something that may come as a surprise to you," Brandon said. "The fact that he is twice her age doesn't disturb me at all. Age isn't that important when two people are deeply in love and have many good years ahead of them. But he is on Earth and she is on Mars. That does disturb me. And it is beginning to disturb her."

"That's what I wanted to talk to you about," Stearns said. "I'm seriously concerned about her. She shuts herself in her room, and won't even talk to me at times. She won't talk to anyone. But I'm sure you know that she is becoming inwardly tormented. No one is in a better position to know . . ."

"Yes . . . the change in her has worried me a great deal," Brandon said. "It has worried my wife. When she is with us she tries very hard to pretend that she is completely untroubled but we're too familiar with her every mood not to see through the pretense."

"I'm sure no one understands her any better," Stearns said. "But still—I wonder if you realize just how close she may be to the breaking point. If she was simply unhappy I wouldn't be nearly so concerned about her, because she's the kind of girl who can take a great deal of unhappiness in her stride. But it goes deeper than that. I've watched her, studied her closely during the past few weeks. When she thought the Station might return to Earth she felt so elated that she even—well, she kissed me, sir. She threw her arms around me and said I was the best friend she'd had and she was going to miss me terribly, because she was quite sure I'd never be content to remain on Earth for long. As for herself, she was going to stay on Earth until the stars fell out of the sky.

"For a moment I felt as if she might really—well, care for me a little. But I woke up quickly enough. She was thinking of him even when she kissed me. In fact, that was *why* she kissed me."

"I'm afraid you're right about that," Brandon said. "I admire your courage in facing up to it honestly."

"My courage or lack of it doesn't really matter," Stearns said. "What matters is the struggle that is taking place in her mind. She can't endure the thought that she may have to go on loving him across fifty million miles of space.

"I decided it was time to talk to you about it, sir. I don't think you realize just how bad it is. You're very close to her, as you say, and she's good at pretending. In some respects she's a natural actress—always has been. She dramatizes everything that happens to her, but that doesn't mean she doesn't take life as seriously as people who keep their thoughts and emotions to themselves."

Brandon had the feeling that Stearns was keeping something back and it deepened the look of apprehension which had come into his eyes.

"Has she done or said anything in the last few days that you think would come as a shock to me?" he asked. "I want the full truth—not just a part of it. If you're wrong . . . if you're not quite sure how important it may be . . . tell me anyway. I won't accuse you of being an alarmist."

"Well . . . there *was* something," Stearns said. "Something she said the last time I talked to her. She said, 'Not even Dad and my mother care much whether I live or die. If I had a serious illness they'd come to me and tell me how terrible it would be for them if they lost me. They love me very much. I've never doubted that. But you can love someone and not realize at all that there are two ways of dying. If you die inwardly even the people who are closest to you and who love you the most go right on pretending that you're perfectly well. They deceive themselves about it, and they don't seem to care. You're still walking around with the same look on your face that you had before— if you're the kind of person who tries to be brave—and they can't believe you're really a walking corpse. Just a lifeless body—walking about and even smiling at times, but inwardly as dead as you'll ever be.'"

"She said that?" Brandon asked. "Are you quoting her exact words."

"As nearly as I can recall them," Stearns said. "She said something else: 'Does it make any sense, really, to keep the body alive? Why go on deceiving the people who love you the most? You're only making it harder for them when they finally wake up to the truth and realize how unintentionally cruel they've been.'"

Brandon tightened his lips and said nothing for a moment. He was quite sure that he had paled percepti- bly, and he stepped quickly back into the shadows that clustered thickly behind the wind velocity recorder, so that Stearns could no longer see what was happening to his face. It was a foolish point of pride perhaps. But he did not want a young man half his age to see him in quite so badly shaken a state.

"I think I understand," he said, finally. "Thanks for keeping nothing back."

"What I feel she needs most right now," Stearns said, "is complete reassurance from you. She has to be made to believe that it isn't—well, a completely hopeless love. It's hard for me to say this, sir . . . because if they never meet, on Mars or on Earth, there might be a chance for me. But I love her too much to stay blind to the fact that something must be done immediately to give her some measure of hope. Otherwise—I'm afraid to even ask myself what could happen. If she gets no reassurance at all—"

Brandon stepped out into the light again and looked at Stearns steadily for a moment. "You do love her, I guess—very much. We both do. So let's not pretend we don't know what could happen if she becomes so desperate she can't see a glimmer of hope anywhere. If I have to lie to her . . . I will. Does that satisfy you?"

"It does, sir. If there's anything you'd like me to tell her—"

"I'll take care of it," Brandon said. "I hope my shoulders are broad enough to give her the kind of support she's going to need. She's a difficult girl, this daughter of mine. You didn't really have to blueprint it for me, but you couldn't have known that. I'd be grateful if you'd go now. I've got a lot of thinking to do."

When the door panel had closed behind Stearns, Brandon stood very still for a moment, his hand cupped around the summit of the wind velocity recorder and his eyes staring into vacancy. Then his jaw muscles tightened and he reached out and removed from its hook on the nearest of the small instrument panels an inter-Station communications disk.

He rotated the disk with his thumb, his face set in tight lines. There ensued a faint humming sound and he put the disk to his ear and waited. "Goulert," a voice said. "Family Unit Section T 7."

"Hello, Leon," Brandon said. "I want you to check on something for me. Has my daughter gone outside alone at any time during the past week? Consult the Section Register and call me back."

"I don't need to do that, sir," Goulert said. "I was just going to dial you. Your daughter went outside early this morning and she hasn't come back." There was an unmistakable note of concern in the Section T 7 recorder's voice. "I don't think it's anything to be alarmed about, sir," he added quickly, in an attempt at reassurance that carried very little conviction. "She's stayed out for as long as six hours in the past, as you know. She told me—I suppose I shouldn't repeat this —that she felt you were overstrict about not wanting her to go outside alone. She's been gone seven hours this time, sir, but when you remember—"

"Seven hours!" Brandon almost shouted the words. "Why didn't you dial me before? Where is my wife? Do you know? Has she gone outside too?"

"Yes sir. About two hours ago. I could see that she was a little worried. But she asked me not to say anything to you about it until she got in touch with me from outside. She took a portable transmitter with her, sir."

"You should have let me know within half an hour if no call came through!" Brandon said, his voice tremulous with anger.

"I'm sorry, sir. You're right, of course. But she told me it might take some time for her to find your daughter and I could see that she didn't want to worry you when there was probably no reason for you to become alarmed."

"You've talked to my wife often enough to know better!" Brandon said. "She'll go to almost any length to spare me because she knows what a strain I've been under. If people would use their heads more—"

"I'm sorry, sir," Goulert said again.

"I couldn't be any more worried than I am right now," Brandon said. "Where do *you* think my daughter may have gone?"

"Probably to the rock cluster," Goulert said. "She told me once that it reminded her of Stonehenge. Of course it isn't anything like as large, and it's certainly a natural formation, which Stonehenge is not. Stonehenge covers an area of ten thousand feet, and when you stand on Salisbury Plain in Wiltshire looking up at it you seem to be in another world. I've been there twice, sir, and I think I know how your daughter feels. An invisible presence seems to hover over it. If the Druids built it, as many believe, they must have known how to bring the Unknown very close."

"Too close," Brandon said. "What you're trying to tell me is that she's far too imaginative, and too much given to brooding. When you're alone in the desert, the solitude can be oppressive. Didn't it occur to you that I might be worried about that too, if she stayed out too long?"

Brandon clicked off the disk without waiting for Goulert to reply.

13

BRANDON stood at the base of the Station, just outside a still thrumming airlock, and looked up at its towering bulk. It was immovable, with a monstrous kind of solidity, but there were times when he could not avoid picturing it crashing down upon him and burying him fathoms deep in an ocean of sand.

What if it should begin to vibrate? What if some sudden shifting about of rock formations deep beneath the sand—a phenomenon not unknown on Earth—should start it tilting, falling?

How could one be absolutely sure that such geologic upheavals were of infrequent occurrence on Mars? The sky was never filled with great billowing clouds of volcanic ash, blotting out the sunlight, and structures did not collapse and go tumbling into an abyss the way they did on Earth in regions where volcanoes were active.

But Mars was the opposite of a dead world, despite the absence of volcanic activity. All of the basic materials of life were present in the soil, including scattered pockets of moisture, and the sky was often filled with fleecy, swift-moving clouds.

Moisture, warmth—at high noon the temperature often soared to almost tropical levels—rich mineral deposits and a plenitude of sunlight had provided the planet with a vegetable growth, in the nondesert areas, more luxuriant than one would ordinarily expect to find on a world where there was so little oxygen in the air that a man could not safely cross a hundred feet of desert without an oxygen cylinder strapped to his back and an inhalation mechanism covering his nostrils.

Brandon had not emerged from the Station alone. In a cuplike depression in the sand just below the airlock, which had been scooped out by flurries of wind sweeping along the metal wall at his back, there was sufficient oxygen to enable him to breathe without the aid of a mask, and to speak reassuringly to Stearns, even though he had to raise his voice a little to make himself heard above the drumming of the sand.

"We'll find her," he said. "We know exactly where to search, and won't have to go tramping on for miles. Quite possibly Helen has found her already and they're on their way back to the Station. Helen has been gone, Goulert says, for about two hours. That would give her just about enough time to get to the rock cluster and start back . . ."

"But what if she didn't go to the rock cluster this time, sir?" Stearns said. "We can't be sure she didn't go roaming off across the desert at random. She could very easily get lost, since she didn't take a transmitter with her."

"She goes to the rock cluster whenever she wants to be alone," Brandon said. "There's something about those great upright slabs of stone set in a circle that reminds Goulert of Stonehenge and I'm quite sure he's the one who is most to blame for the morbid fascination the place seems to have for her. She told me once that she had never met anyone quite as imaginative as Goulert. He's convinced her that the rock cluster can bring her closer to the elemental forces of nature. Perhaps he's right, but I don't think it does her any good to go there."

"We'd better get started, sir," Stearns said.

Brandon nodded and the two men moved out from the shadow of the Station and started advancing across the open plain, walking side by side until Brandon dropped a short distance behind to straighten out a kink in his shoulder muscles.

Brandon's shoulders were beginning to ache a little from the strain of moving so swiftly over the plain against the blowing sand and the continuous buffeting of the wind. For the most part the sand was close-packed and firm underfoot. But here and there the wind was piling it up in drifts, and if he had been trampling in heavy boots through a snowbank on Earth he would not have been forced to clear a path for himself any more vigorously. He had to plough his way forward, and at times his gravity boots sank almost knee-deep into the sand.

The desert as a whole was fairly flat, and he could see for miles in all directions. But though there were no hills and valleys or rock formations projecting from the soil the plain was dotted with many deep, cuplike hollows similar to the one into which he and Stearns had descended on emerging from the Station.

They had covered a little more than a mile and a half when Brandon came to an abrupt halt, waved to Stearns, who was floundering through a sand drift a hundred feet to the left of him, and pointed toward the largest hollow they had so far encountered. Then he tapped his oxygen mask, and continued on toward it. He paused an instant at the rim to stare down, and re-adjust the cylinder on his back until it rested more comfortably between his shoulderblades.

Beckoning to Stearns again, he leaned backward and descended slowly, keeping his arms slightly raised to maintain a precarious balance until he reached the bottom.

He waited until he saw Stearns descending before he took off his mask, and breathed cautiously. It took him a full minute to decide that there was sufficient oxygen pocketed in the deep, cuplike hollow to permit him to keep the mask in his hand without running the risk of suffocation.

Stearns followed Brandon's example, descending slowly and ripping off his oxygen mask the instant the corrugated soles of his gravity boots were firmly planted on the smooth, close-packed soil at the base of a wall so steep that it seemed almost vertical.

He looked at Brandon, smiling a little crookedly without mirth. "You must have wanted to talk to me pretty badly, sir," he said, his eyes sweeping over all four walls of the sixty-foot-deep hollow.

"I did," Brandon said, nodding. "I gave it considerable thought, in fact, before I waved to you. We'll have lost only a few minutes and there's something I've got to discuss with you. It's a little hard to explain. . . . But I'm not as sure as I was when we started out that we'll find my daughter at the rock cluster. And I'm naturally worried about my wife as well. Perhaps—it might be better if we split up. I could go on to the cluster and you could circle around in the desert and search in more than one direction. How do you feel about it?"

"It makes a great deal of sense to me, sir," Stearns replied. "I was hoping we might find some footprints. But they seldom last long when there's a stiff wind blowing . . ."

"All right," Brandon said. "That's settled. One thing more. Every half hour or so you'd better contact me on your transmitter. When we're together the two instruments set up such a clatter you can't hear yourself think—much less communicate. But as soon as we're three or four miles apart the transmission will be crystal clear. Helen told Goulert to wait until he heard from her before he informed me that my daughter had gone outside and failed to return. I'm sure she'll try very hard to get a message through to him—if she hasn't done so already. So we'd better both keep in contact with the Station at frequent intervals, to be on the safe side."

Stearns nodded and replaced his mask, staring up at the almost vertical wall of sand above him.

"You go first," Brandon said. "Be careful now. Wedge your boots into the sand as you ascend, but not too deeply. And don't try to climb out too rapidly."

He replaced his own mask and stepped back, to give Stearns time to maneuver.

Stearns approached the wall, and wedged the toe of his left boot into the sand, raising his right foot slightly higher, and climbing slowly step by step. Brandon waited until he was almost at the top before he followed him.

Stearns was less than three feet from the top when it happened. The sand directly beneath him began to swirl rapidly about, slowly at first and then more rapidly, until almost all of the sand between Stearns and Brandon was in swift, circular motion.

Brandon ripped off his oxygen mask again, and stared up in alarm, swinging about as he did so into a back-to-the-slope position. He was not concerned for his own safety at all, for he had realized instantly that he could slide swiftly to the bottom of the hollow before the shifting about of the sand sent a smothering cloud of silicon dust cascading down over him. But Stearns, he knew, was in very great danger, for he was still too far from the top of the hollow to hurl himself over the rim to safety, and the sand directly beneath him was turning

a part of the slope into a yawning chasm as it swirled
about with swiftly increasing velocity.

Brandon would not have recoiled from sharing the
danger if there had been the remotest possibility of
shortening the distance which separated them before
the disintegration of the slope swept Stearns deep into
the widening chasm. But not only would getting to him
in time have been impossible—there was nothing that
the success of such an attempt could have accomp-
lished.

Brandon shouted a warning as he let himself slide
downward, spreading his elbows wide to preserve his
equilibrium. His own voice startled him. It echoed
loudly in the stillness, each word ringing out like a
pistol shot.

"The slope's collapsing! Don't struggle too hard!
Cover your eyes and let the sand carry you downward!
I'll get to you before you smother!"

Could he do that, he wondered wildly? How deep
would Stearns be buried if a ton of sand descended
upon him before the collapsing slope carried him to the
bottom of the hollow?

The instant Brandon reached the base of the slope he
dragged himself across the hollow to its opposite wall
without stopping to get to his feet. Just as he reached
the wall an avalanche of sand descended, filling the
hollow with a lung-choking cloud of dust as it crashed
down, and grew swiftly into a mound seven feet high.

The mound changed shape as the sand continued to
pile up, growing wider at its base. The sand geysered,
spurting straight across the hollow and spreading in all
directions. It rose as it spread like a gale-lashed,
steadily mounting sheet of water until it was as high as
Brandon's waist. But it rose no higher as it swept toward the wall, and stopped just short of where Brandon
was crouching.

The avalanche had filled the hollow with a roaring

sound. But after a moment the hollow became silent, except for a faint patter as of a light rain descending.

Brandon stood up, swaying a little and racked by spasms of coughing. The oxygen mask protected his face from the stinging sand but he had failed to replace it in time to keep his lungs from smarting and his throat from tightening up.

As he stared across the hollow through the thinning and slowly settling dust a grim foreboding came upon him. The mound was hazily visible through the dust and he could detect no movement from its base to its summit. Not only was Stearns completely buried, but so great a weight of sand had descended on top of him that Brandon was by no means sure that he was still alive or wouldn't suffocate before he could dig himself out.

Brandon knew that there was no time to waste, that he had to start digging too. But for the barest instant he experienced a paralysis of will which kept him motionless. He knew that it was shock-induced—an experience familiar to everyone. But that did not prevent him from reproaching himself for having lost a few precious seconds when the paralysis was shattered by an urgency which propelled him toward the mound with a picture in his mind of a desperately struggling man, gasping, choking, his face a mask of agony as he clawed at the sand that was smothering him.

How deep was Stearns buried? Could a man dig himself out from beneath more than a ton of sand just by using his hands as a trowel and thrusting his body upward? Might not the sand sift out from under him as he struggled, causing him to make no progress at all, or to sink even deeper? Brandon didn't know, and there was nothing to be gained by trying to resolve so torturing an uncertainty. There was only one thing he could be sure about. He had to dig and dig fast, with all his strength, even if it meant digging at random.

Just ascending to the top of the mound made Brandon's heart sink, for he had nothing firm to cling to, and twice before he reached the top he floundered and fell back several feet. He tried again, and this time reached the top without floundering, only to be gripped by a feeling of utter hopelessness.

It was only when he dragged himself halfway across the summit and started digging that he realized how impossible it was to scoop out more than a few pailfuls of sand and reach any depth at all by using his hands. He had no pail to measure with, but he could see after a full minute of frantic digging that the sand that was rising into small mounds to the right and left of him would not have filled four pails to capacity.

Yet he dared not stop digging, even for a few seconds. How long could a man survive, buried beneath a ton of sand? Could he breathe at all? Perhaps . . . if he were not buried too deeply. The sand had just descended and was certainly not as solidly packed as the sand at the bottom of the hollow, or the sand above on the open desert. There might even be a few yawning gaps in the mound which had failed to fill in completely. If Stearns refused to abandon hope and thrust out vigorously with his elbows—

Brandon stopped digging abruptly. Shock could do strange things to the human mind but what it had done to his mind made him wonder whether he had not been behaving like a fool who was also a madman. He had completely forgotten that Stearns had put on his oxygen mask before ascending the slope and must still be wearing it.

For an instant a great wave of relief swept over him, but it was of short duration. The avalanche could very easily have ripped the mask from Stearns' face, or shattered the entire breathing apparatus. If the tube alone became bent or clogged with dust the oxygen in the cylinder might just as well be methane gas or steam under pressure.

Still—Stearns had more of a chance now. It was not as hopeless as it had seemed at first, and Brandon took heart from that, and began to dig again, with the kind of furious vigor which only hope can engender.

He dug steadily for ten minutes and the mounds of sand on both sides of the excavation grew considerably higher, and would have filled more than thirty pails to capacity. He'd been mistaken, he realized, about how much progress a man could make with just his two hands if he set about digging in sand or soft earth with enough time at his disposal. It was something that any child building sand castles at the seashore could have told him, but there were no seashores on Mars, and the thirty-eight children at the Station had never gone romping along the beaches of Earth at ebbtide with the sun and wind in their hair. And right at the moment Brandon's own childhood seemed very far behind him, and if he had tried to recall the brightly painted pails he had emptied and refilled so many times at the age of seven, while the beautiful fortifications arose close to the surfline battlement by battlement, and gulls dipped and wheeled overhead, and a child's will was the wind's will, he would have thought himself even madder than he had been a moment before, when shock had prevented him from remembering that Stearns had been wearing his oxygen mask.

When he had been digging for twelve minutes he looked down into the yawning pit at his feet—he had climbed down into it and ascended again a half dozen times—and a look of amazement came into his eyes. Then he made the mistake of remembering just *why* he was digging, and a feeling of hopelessness crept over him again.

But this time it was a tempered kind of hopelessness, such as a man might experience when confronting what might well become an almost insurmountable task. It was the task itself he felt hopeless about, and not Stearn's chances of getting out of the mound alive. If Stearns were still wearing his mask he could remain buried for an hour, and go right on drawing air into his lungs. For seventeen hours, in fact, if just being able to breathe could keep a man alive that long beneath a ton of tumbled sand, with a dust storm raging overhead and the cold Martian night covering the walls of the hollow with a thin coating of ice.

Brandon suddenly realized that he had deceived himself as to the possibility of completing in a few minutes a rescue operation of such magnitude—bare-handed and without assistance. Without knowing just how much sand had descended on Stearns to dig straight down from the summit of the mound in the hope of getting to him quickly was, at best, a long odds gamble. He could have been buried anywhere in the mound and it was almost as wide as it was high.

Only Brandon's fear that the avalanche might have torn the mask from Stearns' face had kept him digging. But without the right kind of excavating equipment there was very little likelihood that he could clear away the sand over a wide enough area to accomplish anything at all. Just a faint stir of movement deep in the mound might have helped to guide him to where Stearns was buried, if he scooped out enough sand with his hands. But even that would have been a gamble and he might have gone on digging for an hour.

It was a mistake which could hardly have been avoided, for his only thought had been to get to Stearns as quickly as possible and before it was too late. But he should have stopped digging the instant he remembered that Stearns had been wearing his oxygen mask, and returned to the Station for assistance.

He had at least one thing to be grateful for. Bad as the shock and uncertainty had been it was no longer preventing him from thinking clearly and weighing the risks in a realistic way. With luck, he could still return to the Station and be back with the right kind of excavating equipment in less than an hour. It was the only alternative that made sense, for the time factor was less important than what an excavating machine equipped with a locator dial could accomplish if a half-dozen men stood by to keep it operating at peak efficiency. Stearns' exact position in the mound could be located instantly, and a tunnel bored through the sand to the dial-indicated spot in a matter of minutes.

There was only one thing that Brandon was still a little uncertain about. Precisely how long had it taken him to reach the hollow? Fifteen minutes? Twenty? It seemed unlikely that more than twenty minutes had elapsed between his departure from the Station and his arrival at the hollow. But even if he doubled that estimate the Station would still be too near to enable him to make use of his transmitter to summon help. At so close a range any message he might attempt to send would be so distorted by static interference that it would come through on the receiving instrument as a prolonged sequence of shrieks and whistles.

He thought for an instant of trying anyway, to make absolutely sure, then decided that he would be wasting too many precious minutes. There wasn't the remotest chance that he could get a message through and he would have to go and return himself if he wanted to—

He heard it then, a faint, swishing sound, as if the sand in the hollow was being whirled about again by the wind. He straightened abruptly and stared about him. The sand did not seem to be in motion anywhere, and he was quite sure that the sound was not coming from deep within the mound. It was coming from somewhere above him, and it was getting louder.

The sand about him turned darker, as if the sun had passed behind a cloud, and just as that happened the swishing sound was drowned out by a shout that echoed in the stillness like a pistol shot.

Brandon looked up. The men who stood at the summit of the hollow, grouped in a circle above the tumbled sand looked like antenna-waving insects with the Martian sunlight at their backs and a gigantic shadow looming above them which blotted out two thirds of the sky. The shadow cast a shadow, a duplicate of itself, which danced and wavered on the opposite wall of the hollow like the skeleton of a giant thirty feet tall.

There were seven men in all and three of them came sliding down the slope as Brandon stared in stunned disbelief, balancing themselves by spreading their arms and filling most of the hollow with ascending spirals of dust.

Goulert was the first to ascend the mound and reach Brandon's side. He had taken off his oxygen mask to shout down to him, and still held it in his hand.

"It won't take us long to get him out," he said. "He's buried about seven feet deep, your daughter said. These desert hollows have a way of caving in like this when there's a stiff wind blowing. You could have been buried too, sir, and without your oxygen mask. She said you'd taken yours off just before—"

Brandon didn't give him time to finish. So violent was the emotional shock of feeling himself to be facing a threat to his sanity that his fingers tightened automatically on Goulert's arm, causing him to wince and recoil a step.

"How could my daughter have known?" he asked, a look of wild disbelief in his eyes. "She wasn't here. I didn't find her."

"I know you didn't, sir," Goulert said. "Your wife found her. They're both all right, sir."

"But she couldn't have known unless—" Brandon stood very still, as if his thoughts had suddenly taken so startling a turn that he could only stare and wait for Goulert to go on.

"Clairvoyance, sir," Goulert said. "It had to be that.

She saw you and Stearns just before and after the cave in."

"Where are they now?" Brandon asked, his voice harsh with concern.

"Safe at the Station. Don't worry, sir—they're all right. We got here as quickly as we could, because she told us that Stearns was struck on the head by a spinning stone, and is barely conscious. He has his mask on and is still breathing. But we've got to get to him fast."

"You brought an excavator?"

Goulert nodded, gesturing toward the gigantic shadow which loomed above them. "They're starting to lower it," he said. "It won't take long."

Brandon stared upward, blinking against the sunlight. The two men who had descended into the hollow along with Goulert were waving to the four who had remained high above and a gleaming metal cable was descending slowly, swaying back and forth as it swept down toward the mound. The shadow was beginning to tilt a little, and its metal framework was becoming visible, with three more cables attached to it.

"All right," Brandon said. "Take charge and see that they make no mistakes. I'd just stumble around and get in the way. The strain—"

"Don't worry, sir," Goulert said, reassuringly. "We'll drill straight through to him. It's just a matter of minutes now—fifteen at most."

It was a slightly overoptimistic estimate, for it took eighteen and a half minutes to lower the excavator to the bottom of the hollow, adjust the locator dial and tunnel through the sand to where Stearns was buried.

To Brandon the waiting was almost unbearable. He walked back and forth in desperate impatience, half-deafened by the clatter of the machine, his eyes steadily trained on the small circular tunnel that was seven feet deep before the boring came to a halt.

It was Goulert who brought Stearns out, and eased

him to the sand. The oxygen mask was still firmly in place, but Stearns' face was drained of all color, and his body sagged so limply that for an instant a terrible dread took hold of Brandon. Goulert muttered something he could not catch, and started working over Stearns without saying a word, raising both of his arms and bringing them slowly down again.

After a moment Stearns' mouth moved and a groan came from his throat. He opened his eyes, then shut them as if in pain as Goulert slipped one arm under his shoulder and raised him to a sitting position.

Slowly the color crept back into Stearns' face and the oxygen mask vibrated with his breathing.

Goulert waited a moment, then unclamped the mask and removed it. Brandon moved quickly to Goulet's side.

"How do you feel?" he asked taking firm hold of Stearns' arm.

"Not too good," Stearns breathed. "I must have blacked out. The sand started slipping out from under me—"

"You've had a pretty rough time of it," Brandon said. "Don't try to get up. Just stay quiet until the dizziness wears off and your head clears. We don't want you to pass out again."

Brandon was suddenly swept by emotions which were as elemental as the wind which was still blowing in gusts across the hollow, causing the sand to swirl about on all sides of him. A feeling of strangeness came upon him, a feeling, almost, of alienation.

It was as if he were alone on Mars, one man pitted against the elements on an unknown world—one man against a new kind of desert wilderness. And somehow the challenge which that feeling brought with it was tremendously exhilarating.

All of the uncertainties, the doubts which had pursued him for years as to his own identity, even the way the vastness of the mysterious universe seemed to dwarf man to insignificance . . . dissolved like the shadows of night when dawn is just breaking.

Perhaps the fact that he had not been completely alone had something to do with it. He had participated in a shared attempt to rescue, from the hazards of a dangerous, almost totally unexplored environment, a man who, like himself, had to fight for survival against odds which tested to the utmost his courage, self-reliance and capacity for endurance.

He had participated in a staggeringly new kind of cooperative undertaking, for each of the men in the hollow were as alone as he was on the frontiers of the unknown, and facing the same kind of challenge with no familiar desert markings to serve as guideposts. They were all solo navigators on an uncharted sea of sand which might at any moment be lashed by so violent and raging a sandstorm that they would have no chance at all for survival.

In his own mind each of the men in the hollow could hardly have failed to experience a terrifying sense of isolation, even though he was standing shoulder to shoulder with his companions on a familiar level of comradeship.

Human individuality could be put to no greater test under the stars.

Brandon was suddenly aware that Goulert was speaking to him. He had arisen from beside Stearns and was tugging at Brandon's arm, as if he wished to draw Brandon a little aside so that what he had to say would not be overheard.

"You couldn't have given him better advice," Goulert said. "We'll just let him rest for a moment until the shock wears off. He's still a little dazed. But that isn't what I wanted to talk you about, sir."

Brandon nodded and walked a few paces from the slumped figure on the sand. "There are a great many questions I'd like to ask," he said, coming to an abrupt halt. "But most of them can wait. It's my daughter and wife I'm most concerned about."

"I know that, sir. That's what I wanted to talk to you about. Something very strange happened. Your daughter wandered out into the desert and couldn't remember how to get back to the Station. In fact, her memory became a complete blank. She just wandered about at random. She didn't even know she was on Mars. The desert became just an empty, meaningless expanse of sand to her, no different from a desert on Earth. She says it was a bewildering, a completely new kind of emotional experience—as if her surroundings had suddenly become of no importance. Her consciousness, she said, seemed to expand."

"Expand?" A look of alarm had come into Brandon's eyes. "Did she explain precisely what she meant by that?"

"I'm afraid not too precisely, sir. Your wife found her wandering aimlessly about, twenty miles from the Station, and brought her back. She's quite all right now—except that she's badly shaken up, and is running a slight fever. Her memory is completely restored. It all came back just before she had a clairvoyant vision of you and Stearns and the cave-in, sir. I think it was that vision, and not the loss of her memory and what happened in the desert which gave her the worst shock."

"What happened in the desert? You mean there was something else—" Brandon suddenly found himself unable to go on.

"No . . . just the strange way she felt, sir," Goulert said, as if anticipating what Brandon had been about to ask. "That strange expansion of consciousness. She didn't see or hear anything unusual, sir—just had the feeling that she was living in two worlds at the same time, and that it was Mars that had become remote and almost unreal. She said it was as if a veil had suddenly descended on her mind. On one side of it there was nothing but a wide waste of sand. But on the other side —depths beyond depths of light. She felt that in the depths of the light there was a great secret—I think she called it 'a secret revelation'—awaiting her, and that it might come at any moment."

Suddenly Brandon found that he was unable to do what he had never quite dared to do before—look reality, as it bore on his daughter's future . . . perhaps her very life . . . in the face and not shrink from what he saw.

He gripped Goulert firmly by the arm. "All right," he said. "We'd better start back. If Stearns can't make it on foot we'll carry him."

14

"SHE WANTS to see you," Helen said. "She's very calm now. She's desperately in need of rest, but she wants to see you very badly."

"All right," Brandon said, pressing his wife's hand. "I'll try not to tire her. But it always helps to talk when you've kept something locked up inside of you which could inflict an incurable wound. Don't worry— I'm pretty sure she's on the mend. She's passed through an emotional crisis without letting it shatter her, and there are reserves of strength in her I don't think she knew she possessed."

"Sometimes you have to find out how much courage you have by the hunt and peck method," Helen said. "You have to draw it out of yourself piecemeal. But it can come all in a swoop, and that's a discovery she seems to have just made. It's easy enough to be brave when things go right in important ways, even though one thing may be terribly wrong. But when your whole world collapses . . ."

"I know," Brandon said, nodding. "The whole world

135

collapsed for her when she thought he'd go right on being her teacher across fifty million miles of space without knowing whether he'd ever be able to take her into his arms and tell her that at a certain point in a woman's life—and a man's as well—all the knowledge between the covers of books pales into insignificance before the reality of love."

"You'll have to lie to her," Helen said. "You know that, don't you?"

Brandon nodded again. "It's not going to be easy."

"It hasn't been exactly easy watching her grow up and changing year by year, and trying our best to take the place of her real parents," Helen said. "But we did pretty well, darling—all things considered. She's never been able to forget her real mother, and of course I wouldn't have wanted her to. But that has always made it difficult for me to get as close to her as you've succeeded in doing. She doesn't remember her real father and you've been the only one she could turn to for firm reassurance whenever she became deeply troubled. There's no substitute for a male parent in the life of a child. I shouldn't have to remind you of that. She's the kind of girl who doesn't make friends easily, and the few attachments she has go very deep."

"There's one conviction I'm very stubborn about," Brandon said. "She needs you more than you realize— especially now. Don't try to talk me out of it."

"I wish I could be sure of that," Helen said.

Brandon waited until she had turned and walked the few steps to the end of the corridor before he opened the door panel of Betty Anne's room and went inside.

She was sitting up in bed, obviously struggling hard to look as calm as possible, her wavy brown hair lying in damp coils on her forehead. Her blue eyes met Brandon's unwaveringly as he crossed the room to her side.

He drew up a chair and sat down. "I've just been

talking to your mother," he said. "What she had to tell me was reassuring. You *are* feeling better, aren't you?"

She looked at him steadily for a moment before replying. "I—I don't know."

"That's a very encouraging answer," Brandon said, smiling. "A little while ago you would have been completely sure. It means you're making progress."

"Don't try to spare me, Daddy, please," Betty Anne said. "I don't like to feel that there is any need for us to lie to each other."

"Then you did lie to your mother—just a little?"

"She's not my mother and you know it."

"That puts me in a rather awkward position, Betty Anne," Brandon said. "I'm not your father, and we both know it."

"But I feel differently about you, Daddy. I mean—I've never had any *other* father. But I did have a mother . . ."

"I see," Brandon said, lowering his eyes. "Do you think about her often?"

"Very often. What was she like, Daddy? I was such a little girl when she died, and a child doesn't remember too well . . ."

"She was a very beautiful woman," Brandon said.

"Is that all you can tell me about her?"

"You said there was no need for us to lie to each other," Brandon said. "I was very much in love with your mother, and if she had lived you might have been my stepdaughter. But is there so much difference between a stepdaughter and an adopted daughter? I still wouldn't have been your real father."

"But you are," she said. "I've never thought of you in any other way."

"Well . . . there may be some truth in that, I suppose —if you really feel that it isn't merely a matter of heredity. If a little girl has never met her real father face to face or exchanged a single word with him I suppose you might say that anyone who comes along could completely replace him, in defiance of all logic."

"I am still his daughter, even though you *have* replaced him," Betty Anne said. "I found that out today. There's something I've got to know. You should never have drawn a veil over it all these years, hoping that a great deal of it would remain obscure to me. You must have known I'd find out in a hundred ways exactly what happened when I was seven years old and millions of men and women on Earth feared me so much that the abduction of a child did not seem a crime to them."

Brandon's lips tightened and much of the color left his face. He started to speak, then changed his mind and waited for her to go on.

"How much did you think I knew?" she asked. "Not the whole story, surely, or you'd have talked about it openly in my presence. And when I was old enough to understand you'd have taken me completely into your confidence. I know you so well. It would be very hard for you to go on deceiving me—or trying to—unless you felt that the whole truth would make me feel alone and apart, and that I might even become a stranger to you."

Brandon moistened his lips and stared at her unbelievingly. A stranger—yes. But how could she have known? How could she have probed his secret thoughts and put what he had never quite dared to admit even to himself into words that frightened him, because they exposed a dread that had tormented him across the years. A dread that he had sought desperately to keep hidden?

Alone and apart . . . Had he not dreaded always that she would feel herself to be an outcast, and come to believe that he had adopted her out of pity and that his love was a pretense? That alone would have made her a stranger to him, a withdrawn and tormented child suspicious of everyone.

"Well, Daddy?" she asked. "Is that what you feared?"

Brandon nodded without speaking. Then, suddenly, the words came in a rush. "I made no attempt to deceive you," he said. "And if I never talked about it in your presence I felt I was justified in keeping silent. Circumstances had spared me the need of answering questions which I was sure you were going to ask when you grew up, and if by keeping silent I could prevent you from ever knowing—"

He let the words trail off, looking at her almost pleadingly.

But she was not content to let the sentence dissolve. "What circumstances?" she asked.

"The dying down of . . . the hysteria. It died down before you were twelve. The fear that you would inherit your father's gift of clairvoyance was shared by five members of the Advisory Council when the decision was made to abandon the Station. It was partly responsible for that decision and a great many other decisions which followed. The Coordinator System was abolished and new Council members were elected by popular vote. A new kind of governmental structure was established, as you know, and Space Authority became the most powerful governing body on Earth. All references to the cult were rigorously suppressed. Your father's prophecies were simply . . . ignored. So you know what an unperson is?"

"Yes, I think I do," Betty Anne said. "Someone who has wielded enormous power becomes completely forgotten. Even the mention of his name is forbidden. Gradually everyone forgets that he ever existed."

Brandon nodded. "It seems almost unbelievable, but it has happened many times in the past century. A man's name, his personality, everything about him becomes totally erased, blotted out. He is simply not remembered any more. It is a kind of mass hypnosis— a phenomenon which can only be induced when a new governmental structure wipes the slate clean, using every propaganda facility at its disposal to produce an illusion of nonexistence as far as the unperson is concerned. It's as if he had never been born."

"But surely there are some who remember," Betty Anne said. "In fact, there must be a great ground swell of remembrance that only *seems* to have become still."

"It exists, undoubtedly," Brandon said. "And that is why I have lived in fear, since you were a little girl, that your father would be remembered again."

"But why in fear?" Betty Anne's eyes were suddenly tormented, and accusing. "Would you have me believe that he was a criminal with dangerously fanatical ideas?"

Brandon shook his head. "I've never lied to you about him," he said. "He was an extraordinary man, who had the misfortune to be born in an age when everything—all human values—were in a state of flux. In a sense, everything was crumbling and in place of the solid foundations which gave most men and women something on which to build a scant generation earlier, there yawned an abyss. The great system of governing Coordinators was beginning to fall apart. And your father made a prediction that seemed to widen and deepen that abyss. The whole world hung on his words, awaiting another prophecy, a final answer to a question that everyone was asking himself in secret, but that few dared to ask openly. Was man's long tenure on Earth about to come to an end? Would he go down into everlasting night and darkness or survive to reach the stars?

"So great was your father's clairvoyant gifts that there grew up about him a mystery cult that was, in some respects, as primitive as the jungle night. He had nothing whatever to do with the more sinister aspects of that cult, which broke up into warring factions as soon as your father died.

"It was feared that you, a child of seven, might someday inherit your father's clairvoyant gifts. Your mother was also clairvoyant and that seemed to many to double the risks. You became a pawn in a power struggle which once was a threat to your life and that is why . . ."

Brandon hesitated, as if dreading to go on.

"You fear that if I should return to Earth today my father might be remembered again," she said, in a voice so calm that Brandon suddenly realized that he had underestimated her capacity to anticipate what he had been leading up to cautiously, in an effort to spare her pain, and face with courage an indisputable fact—that a child whose destiny is unique may become a woman with the most difficult kind of decision to make.

"The danger would be very great," Brandon said. "A mystery cult can turn the clock of progress backward. We must face the truth openly, in the full light of day. We are just beginning to do that again, and if you returned to Earth now—"

"I know," Betty Anne said, cutting him short. "That is why you have kept the Station's whereabouts a secret from Earth. If I told him where I was do you think that fifty million miles of space could keep him from me? Do you really believe that?"

Brandon shook his head. "He would come. Five rocket landings have been made on Mars, and it is only a matter of time before the Station is located, even though no one on Earth knows our precise location, and it may take several years before as much as a third of the planet's surface can be explored on foot. A way will soon be found of encircling the planet from the air again and again, at a closer range than the orbital trajectory of the previous rockets would have permitted. Now a landing has to be made at once, and we have successfully managed to thwart all short-wave range-finding attempts to locate us by transmitting on continually varying wave-lengths over a wide area. Our televised broadcasts to Earth cannot be isolated on the local level by range-finding techniques, but we are living on borrowed time and only a kind of technological impasse has kept us safe from discovery so far. It could end tomorrow."

"It is going to end tomorrow," Betty Anne said, very firmly.

Brandon stood very still, staring hard at her. Before he could say anything in reply she went on quickly: "You may as well know. Right now I could tell you what he is thinking. Across fifty million miles of space the distance which separates us has ceased to have any meaning. His inmost thoughts, his most secret thoughts, would be known to me if I wanted to probe deeply. But there are invasions of privacy which even a woman in love has no right to resort to—unless the man she loves is in immediate peril, or has told her that he wishes all barriers to the most intimate kind of communication to be swept aside. The day may come when we will both welcome that, eagerly. I would welcome it now, but I am not sure that he would. I only know that I have looked deeply enough into his mind to know that nothing could ever make him stop loving me."

Brandon had compressed his lips. "Then you *have* inherited—" Betty Anne nodded. "My father's clairvoyant gifts, yes. I'm completely sure of it now. It's what you feared, isn't it—what you've been dreading to ask me, for fear that I would lie to you about it . . . and you would have to tell me exactly what you are thinking."

"Do you know that, too?" Brandon asked.

"Of course. I can read your mind as clearly as I can read his. You are thinking that you might have forbid me an attempt to communicate with him in any way—telepathically or on a close-circuit broadcast. You are thinking that all communication with Earth may have to be broken off—because I might be incapable of keeping any promise I might make to you, if the broadcasts continue."

"Betty Anne, I—"

"That's exactly what you were thinking, isn't it?" she asked, cutting him short. "You know that if I made a promise to you I would feel bound by it, because love can command a very special kind of obedience. But you are not going to be that cruel. You are not going to forbid me to go on seeing him."

"Then you will promise—"

She shook her head. "I am going to tell him exactly where the Station is located," she said. "On a closed-circuit broadcast. I could communicate with him telepathically, but a small, lingering doubt might remain in his mind, and I do not want him to be troubled by any kind of uncertainty. Before he takes off from Earth I want him to be absolutely sure he'll find me when he arrives. The long journey to Mars on a two or three-man flight, in a rocket of small dimensions, will be enough of a strain."

"Do you realize what it could mean?" Brandon said, knowing that he stood defeated and could make at best a token protest. Love could command, as she had said, a very special kind of obedience and it cut two ways.

"I know," she said. "You are thinking that if he should break a pledge of secrecy it would put an end to the short time we have left to find out what a new start on a new world could mean in terms of human fulfillment. There may be some great new revelation to come—a final word that has not yet been spoken. That is what my father seemed to be thinking and saying before he died. And you, who are the only real father I have ever known, have clung to the belief, ever since I was a little girl, that I might be the one to speak that word . . . if I grew up without fear and shared with all of the other men and women on the Station a new way of life on Mars. But you have also had a secret dread

that my father's gift of clairvoyance might reopen old
wounds, and cause whirlwinds of superstitious terror to
sweep the world again. That almost made you forget
what you once firmly believed, and just the thought
that I might someday inherit my father's gift has kept
you silent all these years."

"Yes," Brandon said. "It may have been the greatest
mistake I could have made."

"You trusted me in every other way," Betty Anne
said. "Would it it be so difficult for you to trust me now
completely?"

"You mean—"

"I think . . . the revelation will come," she said. "Not
tomorrow perhaps . . . or the next day . . . but soon. In
some strange way I have become . . . a stranger to myself. I will have to become better acquainted with the
other *me*."

A smile flickered across her lips and was gone. "It's
hardly fair to ask him to love two women at the same
time, is it, Dad? Particularly when one of them has my
face and hair and eyes, but will be a stranger to him
as well."

"Only for a while," Brandon said.

"You think he will be able to love us both, even
though he knows that the *me* who is a stranger to him
was born yesterday and can read his secret thoughts?"

Brandon smiled too then, reached out and clasped his
daughter's hand.

"I don't think you've really changed," he said. "A
child's mind is a strange labyrinth, with many hidden
or blocked-off passageways. When you were a little girl
you explored only the bright, sunlit rooms. There were
darker rooms as well, and rooms filled with a strange
kind of brightness which in the fullness of time you
would become mature enough to explore. The gift of
clairvoyance may remain hidden or undeveloped in the
mind of a child, even when the endowment is not un-

usual and does not make a man or a woman as tele-
pathic as your father was. For half a century labora-
tory-controlled scientific tests have established that
beyond dispute. The gift may even appear for the first
time in old age."

"There have been times," Betty Anne said, "when I
have felt that the child's world of hidden rooms was
about to dissolve. Once, when I was nine, I felt myself
to be standing on the threshold of—an impossible brightness. It happened again when I was twelve. I was
afraid, and drew back. If my courage had failed me
completely—and it came close to failing—I would have
run screaming back to the safe, sunlit rooms, for it was
a brightness which seemed to outshine the noonday
sun."

"And you no longer fear that brightness?" Brandon
asked.

Betty Anne shook her head. "I have no longer a fear
of being blinded," she said. "It surrounds me now—I
am in the midst of it. It is like—the sudden opening of
many doors, each filled with a radiance that no longer
terrifies me, even though I have not ventured far into
more than two or three of the rooms."

"And you want him to share that radiance with you?"

"No one could share it," she said.

"You do not feel that even love could make that possible?" Brandon asked. "Is it a path that you must
walk alone?"

She shook her head again. "Not alone, Dad. The
radiance would be even brighter if he walked by my
side. I am sure of that. But there are miracles which
cannot be shared."

Brandon nodded and fell silent for an instant. Then
he said, "All right. Talk to him tomorrow on a closed
circuit broadcast and tell him where we are. We will be
taking a very great risk, but I guess I knew all along

what my decision would be. Subconsciously I must have known or you would have been more disturbed when you looked very deeply into my mind."

"Not too deeply, Dad," she said. "But I knew, I was sure."

15

How LONG, Cowley wondered, would he have to live in a world without hope, performing tasks that had become automatic, a man who could never quite forget that he was a teacher of the young whose pupils were beginning to lose interest in the Earth and the whole of its past history.

They seemed to know that they might never see Earth with their own eyes and had deliberately turned their backs on it. And never once, during all the hours that he remained in communication with them, had they let drop a word concerning their whereabouts.

How could children be so forewarned and pledged to obedience? It had puzzled him for a full month until he had remembered incidents from his own childhood, how his parents had bound him to silence by saying simply: "We trust you. We have secrets in common which must not be talked about outside of the family circle. A family should remain united, determined to stand together against the world, and keep its own wise counsels . . . You must turn a deaf ear to idle gossip and the malicious inquisitiveness of neighbors."

And he had understand and obeyed. A boy of ten or twelve or thirteen could be very wise. And the children on the Station were seemingly wise beyond their years.

It would not have been so bad if *she* had not been like the children in that respect. Not a word would she say, no matter how hard he pleaded with her. She simply would not tell him where the Station was, or how long it might be before every man and woman on Earth shared the knowledge which was being kept from him.

Would it be for both of their lifetimes, and must he abandon all hope forever? If he were persistent, if day after day, every time he talked with her, he renewed his pleas, would she eventually throw "family loyalty" to the winds and tell him?

He doubted it. He knew her too well. There was no longer any doubt in his mind that she loved him, although she had never once said so.

But the agony in her eyes when she looked straight at him, and shook her head and refused to tell him was confirmation enough. She was under a pledge of secrecy which nothing could shatter.

"There is nothing so important as human happiness," he'd wanted to say to her. "Life is too short to justify a moment's hesitation when we are asked to choose between uncertain loyalties and human fulfillment. No one has the right to deprive us of happiness."

But somehow he could not quite bring himself to say it, because although he felt it to be true it went contrary to his obligations as a teacher.

Why did that kind of struggle always seem to be taking place inside of him? It made no sense at all. Basically he was a realist who believed in seizing life by the horns and refusing to be intimidated by the iron hooves of a beast that could be both beautiful and dangerous.

But as a teacher had he the right to kindle so great a flame of rebellion in his pupils? Her pledge of secrecy was important to her, and if he succeeded in demolishing it how could he be sure that she would not be torn apart inwardly? She might even come to hate him.

He sat alone in a shadowed corner of his study, staring at the unlighted screen opposite him, and wondering what they would say to each other today when the screen lighted up, as it would in a moment. Would they start off, as they sometimes did, by talking about things of no particular interest to either of them, to hide their real feelings?

Why couldn't he have the courage at least to be honest with her, completely honest, and to tell her that the closed-circuit broadcasts might have to come to an end, and that as a teacher there was nothing more he could say to her?

Never in his life before had he felt so useless as a teacher. How could he continue to make the past come to life for her when all the glowing pageantry of life on Earth throughout the ages might soon become less than the shadow of a dream in a world about which he knew nothing, and could never hope to share with her.

It was much easier to pretend when he was facing the children. But she had long since ceased to be a child and there was no way of turning the clock back and talking to her as he had when she'd hung on his every word, breathlessly eager to hear more about the Knights of the Round Table and the Homeric legends.

Something had taken place in their own lives which dwarfed the Homeric legends to insignificance, but there was nothing he could teach her that wasn't already known to her. It had, in fact, nothing whatever to do with teaching. It had become so much a part of their lives, so completely the whole of their lives, that there was no longer room for any other kind of communication between them.

The screen lit up suddenly and in the depths of the glow she stood facing him, her face and figure so three-dimensional that she seemed—had it ever been otherwise?—to be right in the room with him.

"I knew you'd been reading," she said. "You just closed that book, didn't you? For about three minutes you've been sitting there thinking."

Startled, he looked down at the book in his lap. He had almost forgotten about it. It might have surprised him more if he hadn't known that there were times when a few minutes could blot out the whole of the past, and make remembering difficult.

"Would you care to tell me what you were thinking," she said. "Or do you want me to guess?"

The steadiness of her gaze made him hesitate before replying. The remote possibility that she might guess correctly alarmed him. Ordinarily it would have failed to disturb him but since she had guessed correctly about the book—

He smiled to cover his uneasiness. "Go right ahead," he said. "I'm not worried."

"Perhaps you should be," she said. "You don't want me to know that if you could you would—"

She hesitated, as if what she had made up her mind to say was proving as difficult as she had feared it might be.

"Would what?" he asked, wondering if he were making a mistake in saying anything at all. If there were the remotest possibility—

"Would take me into your arms and tell me how much you love me," she went on quickly. "Darling, how completely blind can a man be? It's so easy to say, and just the fact that you can't take me into your arms doesn't mean it has to seem unbelievable to you. Did you think a woman couldn't fall in love with a man who's fifty million miles away? If you were at the opposite end of the universe I'd still be just as much in love with you. Wise as you are, you know nothing at all about women."

The look that came into Cowley's eyes made her realize that she had said an absurd thing, for it was the look of a man who knew so much about one woman at least that he could transport her without saying a word into the only kind of world she cared anything about.

"Yes, darling," she heard herself saying. "You can believe it because it's true. Now listen carefully. I'm going to tell you exactly where the Station is. I never wanted to keep it a secret from you and in the end I would have told you anyway."

16

A THIN RED haze hung over the desert, produced
partly by blowing sand and the dull glare of the setting
sun when Cowley emerged from the base of the rocket
through a thrumming airlock and stood staring about
him at a desert landscape that seemed clothed with a
coat of bronze.

From his landside vantage point the Station loomed
enormous. It was less than a hundred yards away,
and it towered straight up into the pale Martian sky,
its massive tiers mirroring the sunlight from base to
summit. The desert was mirrored as well, in all of its
shifting patterns of light and shade, the deep, cuplike
hollows, and distant rock formations giving it the look
of an immense spotted mushroom trampled flat by the
passing of a giant.

He shaded his eyes and stared straight ahead, his
oxygen mask vibrating with his breathing, feeling
for an instant like a deep sea diver who has rounded an
underwater reef and ascended a level plateau of sand

to stare with a wild surmise across a submarine wonderland.

Then he saw her. She was a tiny running figure less
than four hundred feet from the Station, absolutely
alone on the desert and moving straight in his direction.

There was no need for him to speculate as to her
identity. Even from so great a distance it was easy to
see that she was a woman and no woman who was not
young could have been so swift of foot and continued
on without stopping until the distance had been cut in
half and went right on dwindling. What other woman
could have found a way to be the first to welcome him—
a man who had crossed fifty million miles of space
solely to speak her name and take her into his arms?

Nearer she came and nearer and he stood waiting,
hardly daring to breathe, fearing that it might be an
illusion which would vanish if he shut his eyes for the
barest instant, or allowed the faintest of doubts to
flicker across his mind.

It had to be her, he told himself. It could be no one
else. Only the persuasive eloquence which he had known
her to display at times could have prevented her elders
from accompanying her out on the plain to congratulate
a man who had journeyed from Earth to Mars in so
small a space craft, and landed in clear view of the
Station just as the Martian day was drawing to a close.

She must have had to plead and argue and cajole to
spare him the kind of welcome that would have spun
him about on the plain, and substitute a gift of herself
instead.

Instead of thirty or forty people swarming around
him and creating a terrible hubbub they would be completely alone. If another such moment did not come to
him before he was too old to dream he would still remain one of the luckiest men alive . . .

With an effort he controlled his impatience, letting
the seconds it was taking her to cross the last hundred

feet which separated them tinkle through the corridors of his mind like the chimes of a musical clock, deliberately forcing himself to think of them as chimes.

He wanted to shout a warning when he saw her hand dart to her face and rip off her oxygen mask, almost snagging it in her blowing hair. But she shook her head before he could utter a sound, as if she could look deep into his mind, and he suddenly realized that she would be safe enough without the mask for a minute or two.

With no thought at all as to how safe *he* might be he found his own mask in his hand and his arms going out to enfold her.

They did not speak at all as their lips met. For one breathless instant he held her tightly in his arms, running his hands through the tousled wilderness of her hair.

Then he gripped her firmly by the shoulder and held her a little apart from him, and said, very firmly: "Put your mask on again, darling. We'll have plenty of time to talk."

"Yes, of course," she said, already breathless, her chest heaving a little. "All the rest of our lives, John."

He fitted his own mask back on, and very gently, with his forefinger flicked a tear from her cheek.

For a full minute they looked steadily into each other's eyes. She was the first to smile and he saw for the first time just how fair her skin was.

They were both smiling when they turned and walked arm in arm in the direction of the Station, turning about from time to time to cushion the buffeting of the wind.

EPILOGUE

From: THE RAYLE PROPHECIES. Tremont. 2045.

The most widely awaited event of the Martian Colonization Era was the introduction in 2071, on the tenth Station broadcast of that year, of a young Martian meteorologist, Roger Stearns, by Betty Rayle Cowley, her husband Robert Cowley, and her parents through adoption, George Brandon and Helen Brandon

"We who are clairvoyant," Betty Rayle Cowley said, "sometimes like to think that the course the future will take is as clear to us as the ripples on a swiftly flowing stream. But it is not really so. The future is a kind of slow, steady growth and there are no—well, final revelations. All of us—every man, woman and child on Earth and on Mars—contribute to the flowering of the future in a strange new tomorrow."

When Roger Stearns spoke, the meaning of what Betty Rayle Cowley had said seemed to take on an even deeper significance.

"You don't know what it means," he said. "To be

155

the first on a new world. One of the first . . . the proud men, the take-everything-in-stride pioneers. You get up in the morning and the first thing you hear is something better than a lark singing. You hear the wind in the desert trundling the cinders of yesterday's sandstorm. And there's a colder wind blowing down from the mountains, a wind that comes in through the window of your prefabricated metal shack, comes swirling through in convexial currents through the filter mechanism, purified five hundred times, but still laden with the winter tang of distant mountain peaks. . .

"You leap out of bed and pace around in your bare feet for a moment, almost wishing you were back on Earth and could go to the window and look out at a woodland scene, or maybe the sea cresting into white caps, with gulls wheeling and dipping and perhaps a sail on the far horizon.

"But you don't have to do that to feel the morning exhilaration right down to your toes. Because on a new world everything's different and even more beautiful and you can visualize what's beckoning to you outside and how your day will be spent without raising the window at all.

"You can't raise the window. It's hermetically sealed and the breeze comes in through the purifiers, and you know that you can't go outside without an oxygen mask. But that doesn't seem to make any difference at all. Outside there's a big, wide, windswept world that's completely new. You can leave the shack and tramp for miles and you won't run into any wildflowers, or still woodland pools mirroring the interlacing branches of titan oaks and willow trees.

"You can't raise a gun and bring down a covey of partridges, or watch a well-trained hunting dog go leaping through the woods ahead of you with his coat sleek in the morning mist. You can't flick a trout fly out over a mountain stream and go tramping on

*with a big, speckled beauty gleaming in your creel.
You can't even strip to the buff and splash around in the
stream just as if you were a twelve-year-old without a
care in the world.*

"But you don't really miss all of those things very much
on a new world. You should miss them, but you don't, because there are other things to take their place which
are even better, if you can channel your imagination
in the right way.

"It doesn't take too much of an effort, when everything around you is big and challenging and beautiful
in a completely different way. Unless you're prepared
to take some risks, unless the bright face of danger
beckons you on, you'll never know how tremendously
exhilarating life can be. You've got to feel that almost
every precious moment can be snatched from you
without warning, and that it's up to you to live every
moment to the full. If you can't do that you may as well
fold up your prefab and go back to Earth, where there
are just as many dangers perhaps, but where life is
much less rugged.

"On a new world you don't count off your tomorrows
on a calendar pinned to the wall. You just rip off one of
the pages and carry it around with you and every so
often you take it out and look at it, and shake your head
. . . because what has happened to you in a single day
makes a whole month of encircled days seem to rush
together in one blazing instant of time.

"On a new world all of the old confusions, the cob-
weberry distortions dissolve or fall away. You're faced
with a survival challenge so immediate and direct that
you become a different kind of human being than you
were, or even could be on Earth. All of your creative
energies are called into play during every waking
moment, and you are no longer tormented by doubts
and misgivings. You use the whole of your brain,
and not just a part of it, and all of your physical en-

dowments as well. You become totally alive again—although perhaps 'again' isn't precisely the right word, for no man or woman has ever experienced that kind of aliveness on Earth.

Man has always striven for a feeling of wholeness. He has always longed to be in complete harmony with his environment and the men and women who partici-pate with him in the great adventure of life. But that has never been a goal which could be achieved on Earth, perhaps because he got off to a bad start by putting last things first before he discovered how to polish flints or build villages of mud huts. He started warring with his neighbors without really taking the time to look around him and realize just how great a challenge and how exciting an adventure the conquest of nature could be.

"But now on Mars, in the fullness of his days, man seems to have been given another chance. You can achieve harmony with your environment and experi-ence a feeling of wholeness, of complete aliveness, only if that environment is completely new and op-poses you at every turn, paradoxical as that may seem. You must conquer the most formidable kind of oppo-sition to become at peace with yourself, your neighbors and the world around you."

THE END

www.ingramcontent.com/pod-product-compliance
Lightning Source LLC
Chambersburg PA
CBHW031127210626
46816CB00015B/1167